Fran Fortney

3—

The Theft

Betty Gaard

Greenville, South Carolina

Library of Congress Cataloging-in-Publication Data
Gaard, Betty, 1946-
The theft / Betty Gaard.
p. cm.
Summary: Sixteen-year-old Mike becomes involved in the theft of the final exam for his history class and turns to God for help in repenting and confessing his guilt.
ISBN 1-57924-375-4
[1. Cheating—Fiction. 2. Honesty—Fiction. 3. High schools—Fiction. 4. Schools—Fiction. 5. Christian life—Fiction.] I. Title.

PZ7.G1112 Th 2000
[Fic]—dc21 00-038458

The Theft

Editor: Gloria Repp
Project Editor: Debbie L. Parker
Designed by Duane A. Nichols
Cover by TJ Getz
Cover Photo: PhotoDisc, Inc.

Printed in the United States of America

ISBN 1-57924-375-4

15 14 13 12 11 10 9 8 7 6 5 4 3 2 1

Many thanks to Carol Ann Bekemeyer.
Your enthusiastic encouragement
kept me focused and working.

Contents

Chapter 1 1

Chapter 2 11

Chapter 3 25

Chapter 4 43

Chapter 5 55

Chapter 6 73

Chapter 7 91

Chapter 8 109

Chapter 9 123

Chapter 10 139

Chapter 11 165

Chapter 12 179

Chapter 1

Something wasn't right. I stood still a moment when I got to our back door, looking around. It was quiet. Too quiet. My sisters obviously weren't home—no toys strung all over the driveway. No TV blaring for the neighbors to complain about. Even Henrietta, my cocker spaniel, wasn't in sight. But Dad's car was there, and the back door was unlocked. I hesitated before I went in, then walked through the dark kitchen.

"Dad?" I called out. Then again, louder, "Dad?" I could hear his muffled voice coming from the back of our big L-shaped house. I found him talking on the phone in my room, standing near the window with his back to me. "Dad?"

"Mike's here," Dad said abruptly into the phone. "We're on our way!" He hung up and turned toward me. "Michael," he said, then he paused.

"What?" I began to feel my throat constrict. "Is it Mom? What's wrong?"

Dad came over and put his big hand on my shoulder. I was sure he was preparing me for the worst, and I didn't want to hear it. My whole sixteen years flashed before me. I hadn't appreciated Mom enough. I hadn't done much of anything to make her life easier. I didn't take out the garbage unless she reminded me, and even then I sometimes didn't get around to it. I remembered a dozen times I'd ignored opportunities to be helpful. She deserved better.

Dad's voice was a little different. "Aunt Mof's plane crashed in landing. We don't have any details yet, but your mom and the girls are at the airport. They're going to leave for Lakeside Hospital."

"Aunt Mof?" I mumbled, probably sounding like I didn't know who he was talking about. I was so thankful it wasn't Mom that I felt like shouting. Aunt Mof, Mom's younger sister, was coming to stay with us for a week, and I had sort of resented having to give up my bedroom during her visit.

Dad didn't seem to notice my confusion. "We need to get to the hospital right away. Your mom is frantic, and the traffic will soon be gridlocked."

It was a long drive to the hospital, and neither Dad nor I said much the entire way, but we had the radio tuned to a news talk program that kept interrupting with updates on the crash. Hartsfield International Airport is an incredibly huge place with zillions of people coming and going at all hours of the day and night. Now the place was almost shut down because of the crash, and traffic was unbelievable. We passed the airport on the way to the hospital. Lights and sirens seemed to come from all directions. People were standing along the edge of the highway talking and pointing toward a trail of smoke that drifted from the direction of the runway. It didn't seem real.

"Dad . . . ?" I couldn't finish, and he didn't answer. I stared at him. He has a sharp jaw line and a rugged unshaven look. The small strawberry-shaped birthmark on his neck just below his right ear seems to glow when he gets upset like this. His knuckles were white over the steering wheel, and his jaw was clinched so tight that I wouldn't have been surprised to hear his teeth crumbling.

Seeing Dad like that made my stomach hurt. I tried to relax and breathe deeply. Scott, my best friend, always said that deep breathing cleans your insides. I sure hoped he was right.

Dad began to pray silently. I could tell, because his lips were moving. I watched his grip on the steering wheel relax, and within minutes my nervous stomach felt better.

The radio announcer was giving information nonstop now, and it sounded like something from one of those special-effects films. The fact that Aunt Mof was actually in a crash, maybe dead or bleeding or burned, was not a concept that I could take in. But Dad seemed to understand it clearly enough.

I stared straight ahead, thinking about Mom and Aunt Mof. I knew Mom would be praying for her. Dear God, I prayed silently, Aunt Mof can have my room forever—just let her be okay.

The one-hour trip to Lakeside Hospital took almost two hours. The interstate was closed part of the way so emergency vehicles could come and go. Detour signs had cars, trucks, and busses crowding together, trying to merge onto the exit ramps. When we got near the hospital, the street was closed there too. Dad parked the Mustang, and we took off on foot the last three blocks, walking at top speed.

At least a hundred people were gathered outside the emergency entrance, and it looked like the security people weren't letting anyone in. I half expected Dad to plow through them like a tackle at a football game. A guy with a clipboard was answering questions, and Dad stood listening. Mom and the girls had almost an hour head start on us and should have been there. I assumed they had made it inside before the security guys had blocked the door.

Dad saw me searching the crowd and gave a quick nod toward the car. I followed him, running, and soon was out of breath. Dad had two inches, twenty years, and at least twenty pounds on me, and he was in better shape.

"She's not here," he said when we finally reached the car.

I paused a moment to catch my breath, the blue-and-white stripes across my shirt visibly rising and falling. "Well, where is she?" I was getting more worried by the minute. Dad sat drumming his fingers across the top of the steering wheel.

"There were almost four hundred people on that plane," Dad said in a monotone. He didn't sound like himself at all. "The security people at Lakeside said the injured are being taken to as many as eight hospitals in and around Atlanta. Some are small private hospitals I'm not even familiar with."

Suddenly he turned and looked at me as if he had just remembered to breathe. "She probably has her cell phone with her." Then he bounded out of the car and across the street to the McDonald's on the corner. I caught up with him as he was putting money into the pay phone.

I pressed my ear up near the phone. "Alisa? . . . where are you?" he said to Mom. Then he listened, saying "Okay" about ten times. I could hear Mom's voice, but I didn't understand a word she said. Finally, he hung up and turned to me.

"Mof is at Brentwood Hospital. She's in surgery, but she should be okay." Dad stared off into space for a moment, and then added, almost to himself, "It would be very hard on your mom if Mof . . ." Dad let the sentence hang, unfinished. "Let's go," he said.

When we reached the car, Dad prayed again. This time out loud. I leaned a little closer to him and thanked God too, moving my lips without a sound.

Well, Dad finally sounded like Dad again. I relaxed some. Surgery sounded terrible, but it was better than dead. Suddenly I was hungry. I'd have given two weeks' allowance for a Coke and a Big Mac, but no way I'd have suggested it then. I couldn't help glancing back at the Golden Arches once or twice as we pulled away from the curb.

The late afternoon sun was blinding as it flashed off every shiny metal surface we passed. I stared blankly at the walls of kudzu that seemed to shoot out of granite and red Georgia clay. It flashed through my mind that Mom hardly ever passed the green stuff without commenting on how easily it lived and how hard our neighbor worked to keep her roses healthy.

Brentwood Hospital was not far from Lakeside, but because of heavy traffic and the closed interstate, it took us almost another hour to get there.

The parking lot was full, but I spotted Mom's car right away. She drives a pink Grand Cherokee. You couldn't pay me to get into a pink vehicle of any kind. I'd walk to school in a hailstorm before I'd be seen in that thing. Dad and I call it *The Pink Eyesore.* Mom said that's why she got it. So that we wouldn't take off in her transportation. I've only been driving six months, but I can't imagine being desperate enough to drive that Cherokee. I'll stick to Dad's old black Mustang.

At Brentwood, the emergency entrance was less crowded, although there were dozens of people in the lobby, waiting for information. I lost Dad in the shuffle of people for a moment, and then I saw him with his arms around Mom. Miranda and Stacy stood almost between them. The "girls," as Mom always calls my twin sisters, are six years old, and they both have Mom's straight blond hair, just the opposite of Dad and me.

Mom spoke in a slightly shaky voice. "She's out of surgery and in intensive care. Both her legs are broken, but she'll be okay. God is so faithful." We all slumped a little, I think.

While the rest of us went home, Mom stayed at the hospital and waited to talk to Aunt Mof. We ordered pizza and watched TV. My room had been cleaned from floor to ceiling for Aunt Mof. I'd be back in it for another week or two, but now I couldn't find a thing. My stuff had been sorted and boxed and hung up and folded and put away. The bathroom had a big vase of white carnations on the counter. Those would have to go. Maybe Mom would take them to the hospital later.

After only about ten minutes with my Bible and notebook—it was hard to concentrate—I slapped my pillows into shape and tossed back the flowered sheet meant for Aunt Mof. I reached toward the floor and felt around in the dark a moment before my hand touched Henrietta's back. She made a sleepy sound and shuffled closer. I rubbed her head and curly ears for a long time, just thinking. A familiar nagging worry began to descend over me like an invisible cloud. With final exams getting closer every day, had I waited too long to get serious with the books? Our year-round school schedule has some drawbacks.

Tuesday morning was chaos. Mom had come home during the night and had overslept. We all overslept. I tried to beg off school, but it didn't work.

I slid into my desk ten minutes late. "Michael," Mrs. Valbueno said, "we've heard about your aunt. Give your mother our best wishes." I nodded, aware that everyone in the room was focused on me. I was glad when she turned her attention to the whole class. "You have a lot of work to do. The semester final exam is in four weeks, and I know that tennis competition" (she stared right at me) "and other activities have completely absorbed your time and attention for weeks. But your history final must become a priority before it's too late."

There it was again—that cloud—the history final. She was talking to the entire class, but it seemed like she was mostly looking at Scott and Carlos and me. And Amber was looking at me. I didn't have to look at her to know it because I could feel my face burning.

Absolutely no one, not even Scott and Carlos, knew that Amber was on my mind about twenty-five hours a day. Amber didn't have a clue either, but I did manage to exchange glances with her once in a while, and I could tell she liked me. I had thought a lot about how to start a conversation with her, but every time I worked it out in my mind, I ended up looking stupid, so I kept quiet and hoped for meaningful glances. Well, they were sure meaningful to me.

History is not my favorite subject. I have a hard time relating to stories my grandpa tells, much less the Byzantine Empire. I love math, and I do pretty well in science and English, but history is another story. A long, dull story.

Mrs. Valbueno droned on and on in her raspy voice until the bell rang and I escaped to the hallway with Scott and Carlos. When Amber followed with several other girls, I managed to maneuver myself ahead of her so she'd have to walk within inches of me to get by. I was hoping to send her another "meaningful glance," but she passed right by without even attempting eye contact. Her long brown hair swished within an inch of my shoulder. She might as well have slapped me. I stared at my shoes several moments, wishing I was anywhere but where I was at that moment. Carlos brought me out of my trance with a whack on the back and a load of books to my chest. That history book alone had to weigh ten pounds.

"Here, hold these a minute." He tossed his black hair back from his face with a snap of his head as he struggled with his locker.

"Get a new lock," I mumbled, irritated that Carlos was forever shoving his load of books at whoever was nearby—namely Scott or me.

"I'm going to," he answered, oblivious to my despair over Amber.

A hundred times I'd said to Carlos, "Get a new lock," and a hundred times he had said, "I'm going to." I dropped his books in a pile on the floor and turned and walked back down the hall. They wouldn't understand.

By sixth period I was myself again and ready for tennis. I loved the game so much that even Amber would have a hard time competing for my attention here. Well, that's an exaggeration—but at least I didn't think of her constantly when I was absorbed in my game. My game. That's how I thought of it. After an hour of hard practice, Coach McMillin sounded the whistle and motioned us over. His wad of gum shifted in his jaw.

"Guys," he said, talking to the nine of us on the varsity team, "great job this semester. Your record is impressive, and you can feel proud of yourselves."

He paused. Then he said, "However, I do need to remind you that grades count. It takes a B average in every subject to play varsity tennis. But, you know that." Everyone on the team knew that he was talking to Carlos and Scott and me. At least, at that moment it seemed that way. I picked at my fingernails, trying to act natural and unimpressed with the consequences of my sorry history grade, but my stomach was tied in knots at the awful thought of losing my place on the team. I couldn't imagine not playing varsity tennis. It was . . . well . . . it was just part of who I was. There was that cloud again. I had four weeks to up that grade. No big deal, I determined, breathing deeply. I'd do it.

Over the next few days it turned out to be a bigger deal than I thought. With Mom at the hospital every afternoon, I was spending more time baby-sitting and helping around the house than usual. Tennis, though I loved it, did take up time every day. I had homework in other subjects, too, and it was hard to spend a lot of time on a subject I found so boring. Scott and Carlos found other excuses.

On the Saturday after the accident, Mom took the girls to Aunt Shelia's for the day (Aunt Shelia is Dad's sister) and left me with instructions to study history the entire time.

"Don't get distracted, Mike," she pleaded and commanded in the same tone.

"I won't. I'll be sitting at my computer when you get home."

I stood in the driveway as Mom and the girls headed for the pink Cherokee. It was early, and the neighborhood was quiet. Our house looks pretty much the same as the dozen or so other houses on our street, except for yellow shutters on either side of every window and three peach trees in the front yard. Also, towering over the back yard is a huge pecan tree that sometimes leaves shadows streaking down the driveway as far as the street. Dad is very proud of his trees.

I had good intentions as I went back inside, turned on my computer, and opened my book. The last test before the semester exam would be Monday morning, first period. It was important, and I planned to be ready. Starting with the first chapter of the unit we were on, I began making notes. It took forever, but I was making progress and feeling good about myself when about noon Scott came over. Scott and Carlos come and go at my house a lot.

At six feet one inch, I stand about five inches taller than Scott, but like an overpowering hulk he outweighs me by twenty pounds. His short, sandy brown hair sort of grows out crazy in all directions, sometimes making it hard to take him seriously.

Usually I'm glad for the company and ready for any kind of diversion.

"Hey Prickett, on the Net?" Scott asked as he came in. Scott calls all the guys by their last names.

"History," I answered, without looking up. Scott stood looking over my shoulder for a few moments. I could tell he wasn't interested.

"You need a break. Let's sign on—see who's online."

"Can't," I mumbled absentmindedly, typing another question and answer.

"Ah, give it a rest," Scott said. "I'll study with you after we surf the Net for a while."

I ignored him and typed out two or three more questions while he shuffled around my clean room, examining this and that and wondering what was different about the place.

"Then let's go hit some balls," he said, with a tone of finality.

I paused and looked up, and he had me. "Well . . . maybe for an hour."

When I walked in the back door almost six hours later, supper was ready and the girls were at the table. The kitchen smelled like fresh bread.

"Where have you been?" Mom asked, with a tone that suggested I'd better have a good answer.

"Uh, at the courts . . . but I got quite a bit done before I left." I didn't know how long she had been home, but she'd had time to fix supper. We sat down to eat.

"Ready for the test?" she asked, putting mashed potatoes on Stacy's plate.

"I will be by Monday." I was beginning to feel like I was being interrogated.

"We'll be at Aunt Shelia's tomorrow."

I could clearly detect major exasperation in her expression.

"Okay, I'll finish studying while you're gone."

"Sorry, Mike! You'll be going with us."

She didn't look sorry at all. "Why do I have to go?" My voice was a lot louder than I intended.

Mom put down her fork and looked at me a moment, collecting herself and preparing a very controlled response. She leaned toward me and spoke slowly. "You had all day to prepare for a very important test. You covered only one chapter in the unit. There are three chapters in that unit, young man. Three chapters."

I hate it when she calls me "young man." It's like being called an "immature tot." And she had been home long enough to turn on my computer and look over my book and notes. Then she went on in the same tone.

"I'm counting on you to watch the girls and your cousins while Shelia goes to the hospital with us tomorrow. Mof needs further surgery in the morning. I'm sorry it had to be on Sunday." Mom relaxed back in her chair and went on, sort of thinking out loud. "Caroline will teach my Sunday school class, and I need to cancel the dinner invitation to the Lawsons."

My cousins are about the same age as the twins. No time to study there. Besides, I'm pretty dependent on my computer for study.

At least she hadn't said, "No Internet for a week." I wasn't exactly obsessed with the Net, but I was close.

That night, after chores and other homework, I spent an hour more on history before I signed on and found Carlos online. We did the instant message thing for a while before Dad came home and said, "Turn it off."

We left early Sunday and didn't get home till late. I spent half an hour or so looking over the study sheet I had made up for the test, but I knew it was hopeless. I found Carlos and Scott both online when I signed on the Net. I knew they weren't studying, and I found myself wondering how the tennis team would manage without us. I was getting scared.

Chapter 2

Monday morning was dark, matching my mood, and heavy rain and thunderstorms were predicted. I skipped breakfast, heaved my heavy backpack over my shoulder, and left by the back door, muttering something that I hoped would pass for "goodbye."

Scott and Carlos were waiting on Scott's front porch. They slowly gathered their stuff and joined me at the sidewalk when they saw me coming. We were a depressing sight, shuffling along silently, heads down, with only an occasional sigh to break the silence. Doom lay ahead in first period for sure. I figured Scott and Carlos too were wondering how the team would manage without us.

The classroom was as boisterous as ever, with little cliques gathered here and there, talking about the weekend and exchanging notes about the test. My notes were so incomplete that they weren't worth sharing. Carlos and Scott, like me, didn't take part in the hubbub.

Mrs. Valbueno looked especially short and heavy as she lumbered into the room with her long gray raincoat and heavy briefcase. With her left elbow pressing a stack of test papers against her side, she fumbled with her rain hat with her free hand.

"Good morning," she said. Her cheerfulness was annoying. I was just ready to get it over with. "Are you all ready to impress us with your weekend of hard study?"

I caught Scott's eye for a moment and we both let out a silent, if not invisible, sigh. If I had done any hard study over the weekend, I might have been able to smile at Mrs. Valbueno's attempts at pleasantry.

"This will take the entire hour," she said.

I'll be done in fifteen minutes, I thought.

"Put away all your books, notes, papers, and so on."

All my notes together wouldn't help me pass, I groaned silently.

"Face forward and keep your eyes on your own test," she said.

Don't worry, Mrs. Valbueno, I thought. If I looked on Scott's or Carlos's paper, I'd make a bigger bomb than I'm about to land by myself.

As the class settled into silence, she laid a test facedown on every desk. I stared at the white paper, feeling utter disgust for myself and my lack of preparation. I felt stupid and humiliated, and I hadn't even read the first question. The room seemed stuffy and warm.

"All right, class, you have fifty-five minutes," Mrs. Valbueno said. "Turn your papers over and begin."

I sat there staring at the white page, not caring what was going on around me. How could I have been so unconcerned with my history grade all these past weeks?

"Michael."

I glanced up suddenly at Mrs. Valbueno and then quickly flipped over my test as I heaved a deep sigh of resignation.

Name and date? I knew those answers. Great start. Turning through the four pages, I saw multiple choice, fill-in-the-blank, short answer, true or false, and a couple of essay questions. It suddenly occurred to me that I could have had a stomachache when I woke up. I hadn't thought of that. I sure wished I had. I would've had all day to study. I supposed it was too late now to double over . . . but I did consider it for a moment—until I heard Mom's voice in my mind, "Keep your heart and mind pure before God." She had said it dozens of times.

With my face pointed directly down at my paper, I cut my eyes sharply toward Scott's desk. He was turning through the pages too. He didn't even have his pen in his hand yet. Without moving my head, I tried to focus my eyes as far left as I could. I could see Amber's hands and her paper two rows over. She was answering one question after another. I somehow felt proud of her and more ashamed of myself at the same time. I sat straining my eyes for several moments, watching her long brown hair brush against her hand. It was beautiful.

"Michael!" Mrs. Valbueno said firmly.

I jerked to attention, my face burning with embarrassment. She didn't say any more, and I quickly focused on the test. Every question was a labor of wavering hesitation. I was sure of very few answers, and even those questions I was faintly familiar with left me overwhelmed with indecision. I immediately started breathing deeply.

After revealing my total ignorance for an hour, I left the classroom with a headache. Rounding the corner in the hallway, I saw Carlos slam the door of his locker hard enough to leave a dent.

"I'm gonna' be a test pilot. *No necesito* ancient history."

"I know," I mumbled. It was beyond me.

"You know our chances of staying on the team are as good as ice cream in fire."

"I know."

"We might as well quit right now."

I didn't say anything. It was too awful a thought.

Carlos's voice got louder. His dark eyes opened wide. "You know how good we'll have to do on the final exam to stay on the team?"

I squeezed my eyes shut. "Yeah, better than we've ever done on anything."

"No es posible." Carlos tossed the dark hair from his face with a snap of his head.

"Right, DeSantos, not in the lifetime of Methuselah," Scott said.

As I opened my locker, I saw Amber heading my way with her usual crowd of girlfriends. They stick together like a flock of chickens. It sure made it hard to single her out and start up a conversation—not that I'd figured out what I'd say. I didn't attempt to catch her eye this time. I'd been rejected and humiliated enough for a lifetime. But I did listen intently to their conversation. I gathered from what I could sort out that they were talking about computers and the Internet.

Then, clear as a bell, I heard Amber's voice.

"My dad got it last weekend. Here's my e-mail address."

She tore off a scrap of paper and, as she wrote, she read it off slowly. "AMBERDELL." She repeated it as she handed it to one of the other girls.

Glancing over, I was surprised to see Amber looking right at me. We not only made eye contact—she didn't turn away. Finally I looked down, my heartbeat getting louder. It was almost like she was deliberately letting me hear her new e-mail address. No. I was sure she wanted me to hear it. I stood at my locker like I was in a trance. Amber was giving me her e-mail address. Maybe she wanted me to send her a note. *Of course she wants you to send her a note, goofball,* I mentally howled at myself.

Without looking, I was aware of Amber and her flock turning to head down the hall. I waited a moment, and then raised my eyes and watched as she disappeared around the corner. I fought off a big smile. "AMBERDELL," I repeated in my mind over and over. Not that I would or could ever forget. With the last name of Dellaney, her screen name was a natural. "AMBERDELL, AMBERDELL," I silently repeated.

As I headed toward Mr. Adgate's English class with a quick step and a swagger, I began to stand taller, lift my head, set my jaw firmly, and feel my mouth sort of turn up at the corners. I couldn't help it.

That afternoon, tennis practice lasted forever. All I wanted to do was get home and sit at my computer to work out my first e-mail to my girl. At least I hoped she was my girl. I kept trying out lines and phrases and ideas in my mind. Nothing seemed natural. I was determined that the first e-mail note would not be an awkward, bumbling mess-up.

"You're early," Mom said, as I bounded in the back door and dropped my backpack on the floor. She was mixing a pitcher of iced tea.

"Yep," I answered.

"Practice out early?"

"I left early," I said, taking a handful of cookies from a jar that Mom kept out of sight from the girls.

She looked at me with raised eyebrows.

"Well, how about taking out this garbage bag." She motioned under the sink. "And then take the cans to the curb."

"Sure."

Mom paused and looked a little surprised. "You must have done well on that test," she said.

"I'm sure I didn't."

"Well . . . "

I walked out quickly with the sack of garbage in my grip.

The garbage chore actually took only about ninety seconds out of my life. I found myself wondering why it had always been such a big deal.

Supper would be at least an hour, and I was headed for my computer, when Mom intercepted me. "Michael, please help Miranda and Stacy with their art project."

"Art project?"

"A class assignment."

"Can't they color and paste without someone watching?" I asked, trying not to whine.

"Michael, when you were in first grade, I spent a lot of time with your homework most every night. It won't hurt you to help out a little," she said.

"Girls," I yelled, a lot louder than necessary, "get those supplies and get in my room on the double!"

Mom gave me one of her disappointed looks as she began to set the table for supper. I had to go find the girls and turn off their cartoons before they retrieved their stuff from their school bags.

They spread out their colored paper, glitter, and glue all over my floor, and their work was excruciatingly slow and deliberate.

"Just keep working," I said, "while I check my phone messages."

There was only one call, and it was from Scott: "What's with you today, man? For a guy who just failed the most important test of his life, you're acting like you had the points to spare."

I looked over at Miranda, who was watching me silently. "WORK!" I shouted, and then immediately regretted my sharp tone of voice.

She looked up, surprised, but she began to work. By the time both girls finished, it was time for supper. I would have gladly skipped the lasagna and gone right to my e-mail, but that was out of the question. Our family was one of few I knew of that almost always sat together for dinner. Usually I didn't mind, but tonight I minded a lot.

"How was practice today?" Dad asked, passing me the salad.

"It was okay."

"You left early?"

"Yeah."

"Yeah?"

"Yes, sir."

"You feeling okay?"

"Just tired."

"You look a little . . . well . . . different," Mom said.

"I'm fine."

"Mikey failed the most important test of his life," Miranda said cheerfully.

I froze and glared at the little troublemaker.

Mom and Dad both seemed to stiffen. Mom leaned back and looked from Miranda to me and then back to Miranda while Dad leaned forward, his mouth partly open, ready for whatever words of wisdom and reprimand might come to mind.

"Did you?" he asked, clearly already sure of it.

"Well . . . ," I paused for a long moment. "Probably." My shoulders slumped, and my spirit deflated for the first time since I'd overheard Amber's Internet screen name.

"It's that computer. You spend so much time on the Internet that it's a wonder *all* your grades aren't falling." I started my deep breathing right away—I knew what he was going to say next.

"No Internet for a week," Dad said, and my head buzzed with panic.

I focused on my slice of garlic toast. *What about Amber? She'll be expecting some kind of note from me. She'll think I'm not interested.*

Knowing Dad for sixteen years, I knew better than to try to reason with him now. In an hour or so, he'd be calmed down, and he'd listen. One thing about Dad, he's almost always fair, although he doesn't often change his mind, and his punishments can be pretty rough. I wasn't ready to share with him about Amber, though. I couldn't be sure that he'd understand.

I spent the next hour walking around my room, pacing back and forth, and occasionally pounding my fist into my palm. I had to send Amber a note. Somehow, I had to make the contact I knew she was expecting. Impulsively, I sat down and flipped on the computer. Dad said not to sign onto the Internet. He said nothing about using the computer. He knew I used it every day for homework. I opened my word-processing program and started typing, "Dear Amber . . . "

No. Delete that. "Hello, Amber." No, that sounded like a phone solicitor. "Hi." I didn't like that either.

I sat thinking for at least ten minutes. How would I ever get even a short note sent if I couldn't get the first word on the screen? Finally, I settled for "Hey." That had a casual ring to it that didn't make me sound too much like a donkey.

Hey Amber,

I hope you don't mind that I overheard your screen name today.

That was some test in history, wasn't it? I'll need an A to keep up my average. Maybe all that study time will pay off. I'll bet the final exam will be some kind of awful, compared to this test.

If you're just learning to surf the Internet and send e-mail, I think you're really going to like it. I'm online every night.

See you in class tomorrow.

It took almost an hour to work up the short letter. I hoped my mention of needing an A might sound like I expected one, without actually saying it. I wrote and rewrote and kicked myself and wrote again, but the most frustrating part was deciding how to end my note.

"Your friend, Mike." No, too infantile.

"Michael Prickett." No, too formal.

"Love, Mike." No way. (Not now, anyhow.)

I finally settled on just "Mike." She would know "Mike who." I wasn't entirely happy with the letter, but it was the best I could do and still leave time for step two in my plan for the evening. I couldn't send the note without connecting to the Internet. It wouldn't take more than two minutes, but I did need to get a brief reprieve from Dad. I seriously considered signing on, sending the note, and quickly signing off. Dad would probably never know, and this was really important. But, there was Mom's voice again, "Keep your heart and mind pure before God."

After pacing for several more minutes, I walked slowly down the hall, rehearsing my speech in my mind. I found Dad where I knew he would be, sitting with his newspaper in front of the TV. As usual, the TV was on, but silent. It was a funny habit he had, turning the thing on and then keeping the sound off until he noticed something that caught his attention. Mom was busy putting the girls to bed, and the place was quiet.

Dad looked up as I shuffled over, head down. "Sit down, Mike."

I pulled up a little stool and sat. "Dad, about that test." I paused.

"Yes," he finally said, "you really blew that one, didn't you!"

"I sure did, Dad." I watched his face hoping he would understand. I carried on. "I humiliated myself, and I let you down. But I'm determined to improve, big time." Straightening, I went on with a little more enthusiasm. "Dad, the final exam is in less than three weeks, and I intend to be ready for it. I won't let you down again. I promise."

Dad nodded and threw his arm around my shoulder.

"Uh, Dad." I ventured on. "You're right about the Internet. I've been spending a lot of time online."

He nodded again. "I'm gonna' limit myself to half an hour a night." (I had already made that promise to God.)

He was still nodding. "I know you said 'no Internet for a week,' but do you think it would be okay if I signed on for just five minutes a night? Just five minutes."

"Five minutes?" he said. "Why five minutes?"

"Well, uh . . . there's a new, uh . . . friend I met at school," I stammered. "And my friend just got a computer, and, uh . . . I may have an e-mail waiting." I didn't want to admit that I'd just spent an hour of study time writing a letter that was waiting to be sent. I knew it wasn't exactly true, and my face flushed with guilt.

Dad seemed to suddenly realize that the "friend" was a girl, and a strange little smile spread across his face . . . and then it disappeared.

"Five minutes," he said. He stood when I did and gave me an affectionate whack across the back as I turned to go. I could almost hear him thinking, "Way to go, Mike." But Dad was way too reserved to say it.

Tuesday morning, Scott and Carlos must have seen me coming a block away; they were waiting at the sidewalk before I reached them.

I wished for the thousandth time that Carlos could drive to school, but only seniors are allowed parking permits. His faded blue '78 Camaro had taken us many miles in the eight months since Carlos turned sixteen. What was left of the original leather interior had been carefully repaired with silver duct tape, and with a 350 dual exhaust engine, muffled just enough to avoid a traffic citation, we freely roamed the few square miles of Cross Springs.

"What we need is extra credit," Carlos said. "You know, some kind of report on Constantine, or something, like Mr. Adgate sometimes does in English."

"I don't have time to study for the final, much less time for an extra report," I said, really annoyed at the thought of history in general.

"Well," Scott added, "if we don't do something drastic, we'll be serving the little round yellows for the last time after Friday's competition."

Our last competition of the season was coming up next Friday. After that it would be practice for the following season. We played all the time.

We walked silently, probably all thinking the same thing: *We've absolutely got to ace that history final.* I couldn't imagine not being on the tennis team. The very thought of it almost made my eyes water.

As we rounded the back side of the building near the gym, we almost bumped into a group of girls. Amber was leaning against the building, laughing and making that high-pitched girl giggle that they all seemed to make all the time. I used to be irked by girls' silly chatter, but coming from Amber, it was sort of like music. We only paused a moment; none of us were comfortable around a whole group of girls.

Amber had her books hugged up against her with her arms wrapped around them. With Carlos and Scott both watching, Amber smiled and sort of waved in my direction. Well, it was more like wiggling her fingers as she gripped her pile of books, but it was obvious. I wished Carlos and Scott hadn't seen it. I was sure she had read my e-mail and pretty sure that I must have said the right things.

"¿Qué pasa?" Carlos said, lapsing into Spanish. Then, with a laugh he repeated, "What was that all about?"

"Nothing."

"Didn't look like *nothing*," Scott said, wiggling his fingers in a mocking wave.

"Amber has the eye on Mike, no?" Carlos said.

"Yeah," Scott added, giving Carlos a nudge with his elbow. They both laughed again.

I was self-conscious in a way that I had never felt before, but it was good-natured bantering, and I didn't mind all that much.

Mrs. Valbueno was almost ten minutes late to class. The room, noisy with laughter and boisterous horsing around, settled down slowly when she walked in. She had the test papers from the day before tucked under her arm. I hadn't expected her to have them graded in one night, and I really didn't want to see mine.

"Good morning," she said, smiling.

A few in the class said "good morning," but mostly we mumbled and nodded at her. Amber sat two rows over and two seats behind me. I tried to appear alert and mature. I knew she was watching me. I could feel it.

Mrs. Valbueno continued. "Mostly pretty good," she said, gesturing with her handful of papers, "but a few of you"—she paused, and I stared at my desk—"need to talk with me after class."

There was no doubt about who she had in mind. I thought about Amber sitting behind me, and I hoped my hair wasn't sticking up.

"You have barely three weeks left before the final," she went on, "and for some of you the final will make the difference in passing or failing."

I didn't seriously think I might fail history, but I was sure I didn't have the B average that I needed to stay on the tennis court.

"The final will be comprehensive," she said. "It covers the entire book."

I looked over at Carlos. He was doodling little squiggly lines. With much of his five feet five inch height in his legs, Carlos sat as low in his desk as a skinny little fifth grader. Mrs. Valbueno walked around the room putting the graded tests facedown on our desks. I was relieved that my sorry efforts wouldn't be announced to the whole class. She paused as she put down my test, and she left her fingertips on my paper a moment too long. I had the sinking feeling that she might say something, but she moved on.

Slowly I picked up the paper, letting the outside corners fold in. I glanced around, making sure no one was watching, and casually turned the paper over and unfolded a little of it.

Seventy-two. I made a seventy-two. Not an F but not far from it. I quickly slipped it in my notebook as I looked over for a glimpse of Carlos's grade, but he had put his test away.

Mrs. Valbueno picked up a folder, took out several sheets of paper, and looked them over as if she hadn't seen them before. "This is your final exam," she announced.

Oh for x-ray vision.

"There are one hundred questions on this test," she said, "including two essay questions."

I'm dead.

Then she reached into her briefcase and, using both hands, took out a huge stack of papers. She put five or six sets of papers on the first desk in each row.

"Pass these back," she said, brushing wisps of gray from her face. "This is the exam review. Every question on the final exam comes directly from these review questions."

I got mine and started turning through the pages. I couldn't believe it. Page after page of questions and answers. There were exactly four hundred and nine questions. There might as well have been a thousand.

"We'll spend the three days before the final reviewing in class. Other than that, you are, of course, on your own."

Four hundred and nine questions. I couldn't believe it. I was expecting review questions—but four hundred and nine—no way. I leaned over, resting my chin against my knuckles, and heaved a long sigh. I had forgotten that Amber was behind me.

We spent the rest of the hour doing map drills, and then as Carlos, Scott, and I started filing out with the rest of the class, Mrs. Valbueno, from across the room, caught us with her pointing finger.

"Not good, boys," she said.

We nodded.

"The final counts four test grades. It will make you or break you."

Chapter 3

Coach McMillin was pushing hard in practice, getting ready for the competition at Alpharetta. It would be our last major tournament of the season, and we would be meeting experienced players. But we were good. And we were ready.

After almost two hours of hard play, Coach called us over for his usual pep talk and cool-down, which lasted all of two minutes. Coach was well known for his short meetings. He'd call a team conference that might interrupt other plans and take a twenty minute walk to get to, and then the meeting might last five minutes.

As we drifted back toward the gym, Coach called to Scott, motioning for him to come into the gym office. "History," Carlos and I both said. But why weren't we called in too? We were sweating it out, watching from across the gym for several minutes as Coach searched the office for something, opening and closing file drawers, and shuffling through papers on his desk. Finally, sliding his silver-rimmed glasses up on top of his wispy, short blond hair, Coach McMillin held up a single sheet of paper, studied it for a moment, and then folded and sealed it in an envelope. He handed it to Scott, and said, "thanks," as he sat down at one of the desks. Then Coach unwrapped a fresh stick of gum and reached for the phone. Scott came ambling across the gym toward us with the envelope in his hand.

"What is it?" Carlos asked, nervously popping peppermint candy in his mouth.

"What's what?"

"Come on," Carlos said, sounding irritated at the game.

"Oh, you mean this?" Scott said, holding up the envelope.

"*¡Sí!*—What is it?" Carlos said again.

I never let Scott jerk me around like he does Carlos. I'd usually wait him out until his fun was over.

"Oh, just a final exam that I'm taking to the copy room, that's all," Scott said.

I was intensely interested, but I waited and let Carlos dig it out of Scott.

"What final?"

"You mean whose final."

"Okay, whose final?"

"If you must know, DeSantos, it's the final exam for girls' volleyball," Scott announced triumphantly.

"There's a test for volleyball?"

"Yeah, rules an' stuff I guess," Scott answered, tiring of his game. "I'll be back in a minute."

We paused a moment, watching Scott leave the gym. He walked like a sailor, with elbows slightly out like he was afraid they'd touch his belt or maybe like he was ready to draw pistols from holsters carried high on his hips.

Fifteen minutes later Carlos and I were heading for our lockers in the main building when we saw Scott coming toward us. He was lit up like a firecracker. His face twisted in a ghoulish grin, and he was bounding down the hallway like he was being chased, his backpack swinging wildly from his shoulder.

"*¿Qué?*" Carlos asked.

"Not in a million years," Scott whispered, sort of breathless. "You'll never guess in a million years."

"*¿Qué?*" Carlos asked again.

"What?" I said.

"Not now. Get your stuff and let's go." Scott looked up and down the hallway.

We got our books and joined him outside the building. The place was deserted. The tennis players were usually the last to leave campus. Scott quickly moved over against the side of the building where Amber had leaned early that morning. For a moment I remembered vividly how she looked, laughing with her girlfriends and waving to me.

Then with slow, deliberate motions and a smile that spread clear across his face, Scott opened his notebook and pulled out several sheets of paper. With exaggerated motions and the look of a lottery winner, he held up the first page.

We looked hard.

"¡El examen de historia!" Carlos muttered with a low gasp. "That can't be the history final!"

"Yes it is, my man." Scott spoke quietly, glancing around as he spoke. "It's our final exam for history."

Carlos and I both let out an almost silent whoop, and I felt the same thrill of overwhelming exhilaration that Scott obviously felt. But in about five seconds I came to my senses.

"You're crazy!" I exclaimed.

"Shhhhhh . . . " Carlos and Scott both gasped, lunging toward me.

"You're out of your mind." I looked around for witnesses.

"No one saw me," Scott said weakly, as if he were beginning to lose some of his excitement.

"You . . . you . . . you," I said again, furious that Scott had gotten us into such a mess.

Holding the page in both hands, he began to lower the paper.

"*¿Quien?* . . . who . . . has to know?" Carlos said hesitantly.

I looked at him. He shrugged and looked away.

"You have any idea how much trouble this could cause?" I raged. "How did you get this?"

Scott shuffled his feet some. "It was just lying there."

"Lying where?"

"Mr. Fielder told me to take the envelope to the copy room and leave it there. The history final had already been copied, so . . . well . . . I figured no one would miss one test."

"Then we can just get rid of it," I said, beginning to feel better. "If it won't be missed, we can destroy it, and that'll be the end of it." I relaxed some and took the papers from Scott's grip.

None of us had ever been in the kind of trouble that this could bring. I hated to sound like a wimp or a chicken, but I couldn't help it. It looked like Scott was beginning to feel bad too. Rising up on the balls of his feet, he shoved his hands deep in his pockets and then immediately moved them to rake his fingers roughly over his head.

I handed the exam back to Scott, hoping not to be involved. But I was involved already.

We walked home hardly saying a word, but we were all thinking how much easier it would be to learn the answers to one hundred questions compared to four hundred and nine. Four hundred and nine. I still couldn't believe it. I didn't think it could be done.

Scott took the shortcut home. Carlos detoured to the grocery store for his grandmother, and I cut over to Prescott Street to walk past Amber's house. I'd done it a dozen times and had never seen her, but there were a few times that I'd imagined she was at the window. I'd never actually turned my head in an obvious way. But if she ever came out, I was prepared to act surprised to find that she lived there. From a block away I could see the big bushes with pink flowers that stood on either side of her front door. (Same shade of pink as Mom's Cherokee.) The grass was beginning to turn green, like most yards in Cross Springs this time of year, and her mom's white Ford Escort was parked in the driveway. I passed the house as usual, and as usual she was not in sight.

Our house was quiet when I walked in the back door. Dad wasn't home—no surprise—but even Mom and the pink eyesore—her Cherokee—were gone. Only Henrietta greeted me at the door. I squatted down and stroked her back and ears, giving her the attention she begged for. The kitchen smelled good—garlic, I thought. Lasagna, I hoped. Wherever Mom was, she hadn't been gone long. I took a handful of chocolate chip cookies from Mom's hiding place and then headed back toward my bedroom.

The door was open, and I heard the girls chattering before I stepped into my room.

"What do you think you're—?" For a quick moment, I couldn't take it all in. I stood there for a second with half a cookie sticking out of my mouth.

"Michael," Aunt Mof sang out from where she sat on my bed. She smiled the biggest smile I'd ever seen.

I stood there for another five seconds, and then snatched the cookie from my lips. I tried to answer. "Uh . . . hi . . . uh . . ."

"Come join us," she said brightly, scooting over. Her bushy red hair was pulled back, but it seemed to be all over the place. Both girls were with her on the bed. My bed. Get-well cards and makeup and hairbrushes and girl stuff were scattered all over the bed too.

"Uh . . . that's okay," I mumbled, beginning to look around. The place was like a garden.

About a dozen flower arrangements stood scattered around the room, and clutter was everywhere. But not my clutter. A flower-printed bathrobe hung over my desk chair, two suitcases were open on the floor with clothes spilling out of them, and crumpled wrapping paper and gift boxes lay all around my computer.

"Look, Mikey," Miranda said, holding up a blond doll.

"Me too." Stacy shoved an identical doll toward me.

"Oh yeah . . . uh . . . that's real nice," I said, finally beginning to recover.

Aunt Mof held out her arms and motioned me over to the bed. I edged closer. I knew what was coming. She continued holding out her arms and dragged me over with the motion of her fingers. It made me think of Amber's finger wave.

With a really surprising grip, she gave me a powerful hug, and then a kiss on my cheek. I endured it all silently, but I couldn't wait to get out of there.

"Thank you, Michael, for giving up your room for a while."

"Oh, sure," I answered. Actually, it was a major sacrifice. Now I didn't even know where all my stuff was—and how would I use my computer? . . . and my answering machine? I had my own phone line, and my friends used that number all the time. Suddenly, I became aware of the red light blinking on my answering machine. One message. I wasn't about to play the message here, now, with Aunt Mof, Stacy, and Miranda watching and listening.

I stared at the big hump under Aunt Mof's sheet and then looked away quickly. She pulled the covers back and said, "I'm healing up nicely." Her legs didn't look anything near what I'd call "nice." Her feet were swollen, unless she always wore a size 13, and both legs were in big bulky casts with metal pins sticking out at four or five places. It was a little sickening. She waved toward a wheelchair that I hadn't noticed, and said, "With a lot of help, I can get around when I need to."

I began backing out of the room, when I noticed the answering machine again. Aunt Mof noticed me noticing, and said, "Take it with you."

I stepped over and unhooked it from the wall in one quick movement. I didn't want it to look like too big a deal. "Probably just some guy talk," I said.

As I turned to go through the door, I bumped smack into Carlos. Scott was close behind him. I hadn't heard them knock. They stood blocking the doorway, staring at Aunt Mof, and looking confused.

"This is my aunt," I explained, ready to crawl over them to get out.

“Hey,” they both mumbled in her direction, looking around at the unfamiliar jumble of clutter.

“Carlos and Scott.” I gestured to first one, then the other and looked at Aunt Mof.

“Hello guys,” she called out in a light, breezy voice. She didn’t sound sick at all.

“Well, I’ll see you later,” I called over my shoulder as I forcefully moved Scott and Carlos into the hallway.

“¿De dónde vino ella? . . . Where did she come from?” Carlos whispered before we’d moved three feet down the hall. He smelled like peppermint.

“I told you she was coming,” I said under my breath.

“Yeah, but I thought she was in the hospital,” Scott said.

“Well I guess she’s not now!” I answered, with as much sarcasm as I could.

“So, did you get the message?” Scott said, changing the subject.

I held up the answering machine. “This is you?”

“We’re in trouble,” Scott said, in a tone of voice that said, “We’re in *very big* trouble.”

Finding privacy in the house was going to be a problem. “So?” I questioned when we got as far as the kitchen. “What’s the big problem?” I already knew it had something to do with the stolen test.

“That test,” Scott said. “It was her original copy. It has her initials in blue ink up in the corner. She’ll know. It’s got to be different from the others, and she’ll know.”

“Oh no,” I moaned. I squeezed my eyes shut, trying to remember how I’d gotten in this mess. I needed to talk to Dad.

I stood leaning against the kitchen counter, waiting for someone to come up with the magic solution.

"Me tendría que haber quedado en Monterrey," Carlos muttered without translating. His shiny black hair hung in front of his eyes.

"I'm really sorry, Prickett," Scott said, slightly rising up on the balls of his feet. I knew he was sorry. He sounded like he might cry, but I knew he wouldn't.

I thought out loud, "Well, maybe we could get the test back in the copy room before anyone notices it's missing."

Scott and Carlos both brightened some.

"¡Sí!" Carlos said, his voice rising, *"¡Que bueno!* And it's not like we've really looked it over, *¿no?*"

"Right," I admitted, with no enthusiasm at all. "The building is probably locked by now."

Maybe it would be okay. Part of me wanted to tell Dad—even though there would be a price to pay. Part of me said, "Just return the test and forget it."

"Okay, so we do it in the morning," Scott said.

"We?" I snapped. "The three of us march in the principal's office and say, 'Excuse me, Mr. Fielder, but I believe Scott accidentally walked out of here with the history exam last night!' I don't think so."

"Okay, so Scott does it alone," Carlos said. "Scott took it out; Scott takes it back in."

That was settled. It was decided that we'd better leave for school about thirty minutes early the next morning.

The "eyesore" pulled in the driveway as Scott and Carlos reached the sidewalk. Mom came in with a bag of groceries and then immediately took the lasagna out of the oven. But I had lost my appetite.

After Mom disappeared toward the back of the house, Henrietta followed me as I wandered around for a few minutes wondering where all my stuff had been put this time. I still had the answering machine in my hand when a light flashed on in my brain: The phone message Scott had left. What exactly had he said, and was Aunt Mof in the room when he left the message? I had to find a phone jack right away.

I wandered back to Mom and Dad's bedroom and couldn't help noticing, even in the dim light, how the room revealed their personalities. Mom had the blue-and-white striped bedspread perfectly in place, about an inch from the floor along the side of the bed. Mom's dresser top was completely bare except for her Bible and a small notebook.

Contrasting that, and true to form, Dad's chest of drawers was littered with business cards, spare keys, coins, pens and pencils, and an assortment of sales receipts. His blue flannel pajamas stuck out the top drawer an inch or two. Like me, Dad wore flannel summer and winter.

On the wall next to the window was a picture of Mom and Dad at their wedding twenty-two years ago. Looking at Dad was almost like looking in the mirror, his wavy hair a shade lighter back then.

I plugged the machine into the outlet, held my breath, and pushed "play." After a long intro of the outgoing message and a lot of beeps, I heard Scott say, "Mike? . . . Mike . . . pick up . . . Mike, we're in trouble. I think I got the original copy. She'll know for sure. Call me as soon as you get in." More than his words, it was his tone of voice that said, "major problem here."

I listened to the recording again, watching for Mom to come down the hall and trying to decide how much Aunt Mof might have figured out from hearing the message . . . if she was there when the message came in. I'd have to find out. All at once I heard Mom's voice in my mind again, "Two wrongs don't make a right." I'd heard her say it a million times. Taking the test was wrong, but sneaking it back in would probably be wrong too. Probably. But maybe not. Maybe it would be a quick and easy way out of the mess Scott had gotten us into. I couldn't think about it anymore.

I erased the tape, unplugged the answering machine, and stood thinking a moment. I wouldn't be able to use it as long as I was out of my room, so I reached down and slid it far under Mom's side of the bed just as I heard Dad coming in the back door.

Supper that night was kind of awkward. Aunt Mof couldn't come to the table, and Mom didn't want her to have to eat alone, so Stacy and Miranda were allowed to take their plates to her room. I found myself sitting at the table alone with my parents. Conversation was almost formal.

"Did you have a good day?" Dad said.

"Yeah," I mumbled, thinking, *If only you knew.*

"Yeah?" he repeated.

"Yes, sir." *Yes, Dad,* I thought, *I'm about to fail history, and Scott and Carlos and I have a stolen test that we're trying to return. Thanks for asking.*

"Ready for the tournament Friday?" he asked.

"I guess we're ready." And then I thought . . . if we're still on the team.

"I can make time for a workout Thursday afternoon," Dad said.

Dad had coached me at tennis since I was old enough to hold a racket. I'd never won a set or a match against him. It was a victory to win an occasional game.

"Doesn't Mof look good?" Mom said, looking at Dad.

I couldn't help wondering how long it would be before Aunt Mof left, but I couldn't imagine how they got her in the house with those pins in her legs, much less how they would get her all the way back to Cleveland.

Mom took dessert and a pitcher of iced tea back to Aunt Mof, and Dad and I were left to ourselves. His mind was miles away—in some business deal, I suppose. Dad is a small business consultant in Cross Springs. He meets with customers who need help reorganizing business finances, and then he spends hours and hours at the computer—working out the details. Anyhow, I was relieved not to have to think up conversation.

Before the kitchen was cleaned up a while later, Mom sent me back to collect the plates and serving trays from Aunt Mof and the girls.

I stepped into the room feeling a little shy and awkward. "You finished?" I said, and then I saw that they had been finished for some time.

"Thank you, Michael," Aunt Mof said, handing me her tray. The girls climbed off the bed and carried their trays toward the door. "Michael." Aunt Mof looked toward a gift wrapped in blue paper that sat on my computer table. "Come back in a little while."

The package was about the size of a large book. It probably was a book, I concluded, without much enthusiasm. But I nodded and carried her tray to the kitchen.

I had to dry the dishes and carry out the garbage before I was free to go check out my gift. It was no big deal, but the least I could do was show polite interest. I didn't have time for any more books.

"Ahhh," Aunt Mof said as I walked into my room. She motioned to me to come closer. I wasn't going to get too close this time, but I did move in some. She had the gift on the bed next to her pillow.

Holding it out, she said, "I hope you'll enjoy this."

I took the package and started tearing the paper off slowly and deliberately. It wasn't heavy enough to be a book. That was a relief. Glancing over at Aunt Mof several times before I got the paper off, I could see that she was watching my every move, waiting for me to light up, thrilled with whatever she had brought me.

I did light up—and it wasn't on purpose. The end of the box said, "Compact CD Player." It was exactly the small portable CD player that I had wanted for a long time.

"Your mom gave me a clue," Aunt Mof said after I did all the thank-you stuff.

I stepped closer and allowed myself to be hugged. I didn't mind.

"Sit a minute, please," Aunt Mof said, pushing her red hair back from her face.

I sat.

"Michael, I'm sure this is very inconvenient for you, and I want you to know how much I appreciate your sacrifice."

I felt a little better about her already.

"You must use your computer a lot," she said, waving in the direction of my desk.

I nodded, waiting for her to go on.

"Please come and go in this room anytime at all. I want you to," she said.

I must have looked doubtful because she quickly went on.

"No, I mean it. I'll feel terrible if you let me interrupt your routine any more than necessary. I know you have Internet friends too. Your mom told me. So do I," she said, pointing to a black case on the floor.

She kept pointing until I realized she was telling me to bring it over. I unzipped the bag and handed her a laptop that had to be twice as fast as my fairly up-to-date PC. I was impressed. Mom knew how to check my homework on the word processor, but Mom didn't have a clue about the Internet.

"This is a huge room," Aunt Mof said, waving from corner to corner. "You can keep your privacy on your computer."

I guessed I could. The bed had to be fifteen feet from the computer.

"I'm sorry about your telephone and answering machine, though."

I shrugged like it didn't matter, wondering again if she had been there when Scott left his stupid message. I sure couldn't ask. She asked me to help her with the cables on her laptop, saying she had some letters to write, and then she insisted I turn on my computer and do homework, or check my e-mail, or whatever I needed to do.

Aunt Mof balanced her laptop on the sheet that covered the bulky casts on her legs, and in a few minutes she was busy with her letters, not once looking up or watching me clear away her stuff from my computer table. Stacy and Miranda had probably spent the afternoon in my room, entertaining and being entertained—and making a mess.

I typed in my password and waited to log onto the Net.

"You have mail," the speakers sounded.

I clicked my mouse button and up popped my selection of mail. There was always a lot of junk mail to delete. But there, in the middle of a bunch of advertisements, right away I saw AMBERDELL. Without meaning to, I stiffened a little and looked over toward Aunt Mof. She never stopped typing. I clicked the mouse and waited to see how Amber had answered my first e-mail.

Hey Mike. She started just like I had.

What a surprise to get a note from you. Yes, I just got online Monday, and it really is fun to get e-mail from friends. That history test was really hard. I'm sure you did great. I didn't do as well as I had hoped.

Yeah, I thought, you probably made a 98 instead of a 100.

I continued reading. "*I'm looking forward to the youth rally Sunday night. Most of the kids will be at Michelle's house afterward. Maybe I'll see you there.*"

Michelle's house? No one had told me. I hadn't been to the evening youth program at church in two weeks, and I didn't know Amber was going now. It sort of sounded like she really wanted to see me there. She signed the note like I had. Just her name. I read the short letter about five times, completely forgetting about Aunt Mof.

Suddenly the phone rang, bringing me out of my happy trance.

"Hello," I answered, trying to hold my voice down, and feeling self-conscious about talking to one of my friends in front of Aunt Mof. "Martha? No, sorry, there's no—"

"Hey," Aunt Mof motioned to me, "over here."

I felt my face flush. I should have remembered that her name is really Martha. I took her the phone and then signed off the computer. As I stepped out of the room, I waved good night, and started to shut the door.

"Michael," she called, covering the mouthpiece with her hand, "please leave the door open—always open—and come in here *anytime!*"

I almost thought I could.

Mom had the sofa in the family room all made up for me, and a box with my stuff in it was on the floor. Henrietta was sprawled out on my bed.

"Sleeping in the house tonight, Henrietta?" I said, patting her head and stroking her back.

Dad was usually in his lounge chair by now, but he spent the evening at the kitchen table with his newspaper all spread out. I flipped on the lamp, turned on the TV, turned off the sound, pushed Henrietta to the floor, and flopped down on the sofa. I stared at the TV for a while before I picked up the history study sheet. Four hundred and nine review questions. At least the answers were there. Not possible, I thought again. I read through every one of the questions, making a little check mark next to the ones that I was sure I already knew. There weren't many checks when I finished.

After about forty-five minutes I turned off the lamp and settled on my back, as I stared up at the ceiling and watched the flickering lights and shadows of the TV. I couldn't help thinking how much easier it would be to learn the one hundred questions on the test Scott had hidden away. Even a quick cram session before we returned the paper would help a lot. I'll admit I was seriously considering it, but in our family, the word *integrity* is discussed a lot. I couldn't imagine Mom or Dad cheating—not under any circumstances. I'd been a Christian long enough to know that temptation isn't a sin unless I allow the tempting thought to fester and grow. I had to decide what I was going to do. Dad would have said, "Talk to the Lord about it," but I couldn't, not now. I was pretty sure that if I told Scott and Carlos that I thought it would be okay to copy the papers before we returned them, they would go along with the idea.

I imagined how proud Dad would be if I made an A on the final. But then, I imagined how disgusted I'd be with myself—not to mention what it would do to my relationship with God. Mostly I was really mad at Scott for getting us into this mess and forcing me to choose.

The next morning we got to the back side of the gym before Coach unlocked the doors. The teachers' parking lot was full, and we knew the teachers and staff would be in the cafeteria for the regular Wednesday morning meeting. But they wouldn't be there long.

"Got the test?" Carlos asked Scott.

"No, dummy, I left it on the kitchen table."

Scott was wired and nervous. We were all wired and nervous.

"Come on," I whispered, glancing around. I felt lightheaded. We walked slowly toward the main building, pausing to stand and talk casually when a car pulled up to let out two students.

The dimly lit main hall was empty, but we knew that within ten minutes there would be students everywhere. Standing near the office door, Carlos fooled around with the lock on someone's locker, trying to look like we had business there. Scott took out the test, folded it over without creasing the paper, and leaned over to look through the glass in the office door. The place was empty, but the door wasn't locked.

"We'll be at the lockers," I whispered.

Scott just stared at me.

"Go on," Carlos urged, motioning toward the door with a jerk of his shoulder.

Scott just stared at me.

"You took it out; you take it back." I was feeling that familiar panic.

Scott rose slightly up on his toes. We had only a few minutes left.

"Give it to me," I muttered, and snatched the paper out of his hand.

I rolled it up loosely, glanced down the hall in both directions, and without looking at either Scott or Carlos, I opened the door to the office and went in.

Behind the front office area, Mr. Fielder's office was on the left and the copy room on the right. I moved quickly around the secretary's desk and stepped into the copy room. It was mostly dark with only a little light coming from the miniblinds covering the only window. A tall wooden filing cabinet with boxes piled on top blocked most of the window. On my right were floor-to-ceiling cabinets. To my left were two metal filing cabinets—one blue and one yellow—and a table where the copy machine sat. Between the filing cabinet and the copy machine was a door that probably opened into Mr. Fielder's office.

Scott had said that the history exams were in a tray on top of the blue file cabinet. I unrolled the papers in my hand, smoothed them out, and in two steps I reached the blue cabinet. I started to place the test back in the tray on top, but the tray was empty. I froze, looking around for another tray. No other trays. "Oh no, no, no . . . " I groaned, thinking of Scott. Probably Mrs. Valbueno had already come for the copied tests.

I stood in the semidarkness, my mind whirling. Maybe she'd think the aide who copied the test had lost the original. Or maybe it could have fallen behind the file cabinet. That sounded like a possibility.

It had only been about two minutes since I left Scott and Carlos in the hallway. I knew they were standing at our lockers trying to look casual, but they were sweating it out. Let them sweat.

I reached over the file cabinet and let the test fall to the floor. It landed and spread out its three pages so that one stuck out almost six inches to the side of the cabinet and in front of the door. I picked it up and tried again, this time tossing it in from the side. It landed so far over that no one would believe that it just happened to fall off the back side. I tiptoed around to the other side and picked it up again.

I paused, and put my ear to the door to listen. In that moment, someone came in the outer office. I stood paralyzed.

"Are you sure?" Mr. Fielder's muffled voice asked.

"I've checked all over the room, both last night and this morning," a raspy voice answered. It was Mrs. Valbueno.

"Maybe it fell behind the file cabinet." Mr. Fielder said.

"I looked."

"On the floor?" he suggested, his voice getting louder as they moved closer to the copy room door.

"It's not in there," she said resolutely.

Suddenly a hand was resting on the doorknob as they spoke, and Mr. Fielder's huge shadow filled the opaque glass of the door.

"Oh God, help me," I whispered. "Oh God, please." There was only one way out. With my heart pounding like I might have a stroke, I opened the other door and stepped into Mr. Fielder's private office. It was cold, almost dark, and kind of spooky. The desk was huge and piled with stacks of folders and large brown envelopes. Family pictures covered one corner of the desk, and the chair looked like something the president might use. It must have been a hundred years old.

Behind the desk was a door to the outside. I had forgotten it was there, and for a moment I couldn't place exactly where it might come out. But I had no choice. I bounded silently across the room and out the door as fast as I could. I found myself in the teachers' parking lot, within three feet of Mr. Fielder's big white ten-year-old Lincoln.

I had to force myself not to run—not to look guilty. Breathing deeply and moving as casually as I could, I rounded the corner of the building and, instead of turning toward the entrance where our lockers were, I headed for the gym. It had only been seven or eight minutes since Scott and Carlos and I had passed by there. I sat on the steps and tried to relax. Mom's voice rang through my mind, "Two wrongs don't make a right."

It was only then, sitting on the steps trying to control my breathing, that I noticed my hands. I had gripped the rolled-up history exam in my sweaty palms until it was almost torn in half. I hung my head between my knees.

Chapter 4

I walked into class almost fifteen minutes late. Mrs. Valbueno came in just seconds later. I looked straight ahead, ignoring Scott and Carlos, and not once thinking of Amber.

It was Wednesday, so we must have reported on current events, but I might as well have been on the tennis courts for all I got out of class. About five minutes before the end of class, Mrs. Valbueno answered a knock at the door, and then turned and motioned for Scott to join her in the hall. I thought I couldn't take much more, but here came another blow. The door stood open a crack, and I could see Scott in the shadow of Mr. Fielder's tall dark frame. Scott looked pathetic, like he was standing in front of a firing squad. I felt sorry for him. He shook his head from side to side a couple of times and gave a palms up shoulder-lifting shrug once or twice. It didn't look like he was confessing to anything. I wasn't breathing very well by the time the bell rang.

"¿Qué te preguntaron?" Carlos whispered the moment we met at our lockers.

Scott stared at him.

"What did they ask you?" Carlos repeated.

Scott looked pretty cool now that it was over, but he sure hadn't looked cool during the interrogation. "Mr. Fielder just came right out and asked if I had seen the history exam when I delivered the envelope for Coach McMillin."

Carlos and I looked at each other, wondering why we weren't on the way to juvenile hall.

"And?" Carlos said impatiently.

"And I said, 'Yes, I had seen it in the tray.' "

"You said 'Sí?' " Carlos said in disbelief.

"Yep."

"And then?" I gasped.

"And then he asked if I had any idea how it might have left the copy room."

It was hard dragging information out of Scott.

"So," he continued, "I asked if it was missing, since he was hinting that it was. And then I suggested he should look around the floor or behind the tray or somewhere. But, of course, they had already looked all those places."

Seemed like Scott really was cool under pressure. But, suddenly he stiffened and burst out, "It wasn't there an hour ago, and now it is!"

"And now it's not," I corrected. Carlos and Scott both looked at me, then glanced around and leaned in a little closer.

I told them everything.

At noontime, in the courtyard, I announced, "I'm going to talk to my dad."

Scott stood. "Come on, man; let's just wait a while." He gripped his sandwich until it almost tore in half.

"Yeah," Carlos said. "Maybe nothing will come of it." He leaned closer. "Please."

I didn't answer.

For the rest of the day, I didn't feel very well. I'd have checked out at the office and gone home, but I didn't have anywhere to go. My room had been taken over with flowers and lady stuff, and the family room where I'd be sleeping wasn't very private. I just wasn't up to having Mom fuss over me and ask questions.

The house was locked when I got home. I found the hidden key and unlocked the kitchen door. The place was quiet and dark.

Usually by the time I came in from practice, something was in the oven, but not today. I went to the family room and crashed. After putting the sound of brass in my new CD player and adjusting the earphones, I laid back on the sofa and stared blankly at the ceiling for a long time. I listened to trumpets and saxophones. Turning the music up helped drown out my thoughts, but it would take more than that to keep a B average in history. But the history grade was minor compared to the stolen test.

I felt a thump on my chest and was startled out of my daydreaming.

"Mikey's home," Miranda shouted, her blond hair dangling in my face. Her book, still in her two hands, was resting against my chest.

"I can't read to you now," I said.

"Aunt Mof already did."

I adjusted the earphones and tried to ignore her.

"We can order pizza now." She shouted over the music that poured into my ears.

I sat up and turned off the CD player.

We hardly ever order pizza unless Mom is away for the evening. I wasn't hungry, but I did wonder why Mom was out. I let Miranda lead me back to my room where we found Aunt Mof on the bed, reading to Stacy. I figured Aunt Mof had to have superhuman patience. Miranda ran and jumped on the bed. I winced, thinking of the pins in the casts on Aunt Mof's legs. She didn't seem to notice, though.

"Ahhh, Michael," Aunt Mof said. "You're home."

I'd been home for half an hour, but I just stood, looking around at how my room had changed. The only things that looked the same were the posters on the wall.

"Uh, yeah, yes. Where's Mom?" It wasn't like her to be gone in the evening.

For just a second, there was a change in Aunt Mof's usual smiling expression. It disappeared, but I had seen it, and I couldn't help wondering what it had to do with Mom being out.

"She and your dad are at a meeting with some business people," she said, and then she changed the subject. "You ready to order pizza?"

I ordered, and later the four of us sat around my room and ate. It was the most time I had spent with Aunt Mof since she had arrived, and I learned a lot of stuff about her that I hadn't known before.

Aunt Mof wasn't married anymore. Uncle George had left years ago. I was never told any details, but after getting to know her, I couldn't imagine that anyone wouldn't like to be with her.

"Miranda. Stacy," Aunt Mof said, pulling the girls over for a hug, "run get your pajamas and take your bath in here tonight." The girls instantly looked over at me, expecting a protest, but I kept my mouth shut.

"I suppose you have work to do on your computer," she said, adjusting her pillows and scooting up a little straighter in the bed. A splattering of brown freckles covered Aunt Mof's hands, and wild wisps of bright red hair escaped from the reading glasses that rested on top of her head and held back most of the hair.

I got up to flip on the computer, and Aunt Mof reached for her Bible. After logging onto the Internet, I checked my e-mail. None. That was unusual. I still hadn't answered Amber's note. It was hard to concentrate on anything without the shadow of the stolen test clouding my thoughts. There hadn't been ten minutes since I escaped Mr. Fielder's office that I hadn't relived the minutes I had been there.

I had to answer Amber's note. She was probably wondering why she hadn't already heard from me. With very little emotion I typed, "Hey Amber," Then I sat. I sat thinking and waiting for inspiration or ideas, or even a thought worth putting into print. It was a pathetic effort, but eventually I wrote something that would have to do for now. I'd do better next time. I sent the e-mail.

The girls were making plenty of noise in the bathroom, splashing water and laughing and giggling. I kept expecting a flood to come seeping under the door.

I signed off the Net and took my history study sheets out of my backpack. I didn't know how to even begin studying those questions. Looking at the paper, I heaved a long, heavy sigh and soon my focus was not on the words, but on the terrible experiences of the morning. Over and over I dragged my attention back to the review sheet, breathing soft sighs now and then.

"Stacy says you have a pretty rough history exam to study for," Aunt Mof said, laying down her Bible.

"Yeah." I sighed again. "And I'll lose my place on the tennis team if I don't make just about perfect on it."

"Mmmmm," she said. "Sounds like you could use some help."

She looked at me with her head tipped to one side a little, obviously waiting for me to accept the offer. It seemed hopeless to expect any kind of help to make a difference. But she was waiting, and to say "No, thanks," seemed rude.

I paused a moment, looked from my handful of papers to the only real help I had been offered, and then walked over and handed her the pages. She slowly turned through one page after another, finally letting out a long whistle of amazement at the end.

"I have three weeks," I said. "It's just not possible."

"Oh, it's totally possible," she said. "In fact, I haven't the slightest doubt that you can learn the answer to every question here in less than three weeks."

It was a faint encouragement that I wanted to grab hold of and not let go.

"Well . . . ?" I paused, then finally blurted out, "But how?"

Stacy and Miranda opened the bathroom door about that time, and Aunt Mof leaned back, smiling at me. The bathroom was a wet mess, and each of the girls must have used at least three towels.

The mirror was thick with mist, and the bathtub was full of toys that I hadn't seen before.

Looking at her watch, Aunt Mof said, "Michael, how about tucking the girls in?" I nodded, and she gave the review sheets a slight wave in my direction, then slipped them into her Bible. I didn't have the energy to concentrate on the questions anyhow.

A few minutes later as I stood ready to turn out the lights, Stacy said, "Mikey, you have to pray with us." The girls sat cross-legged on their beds in their pink nightshirts.

"You can pray with each other," I answered with some irritation. I was just realizing how tired I was.

"No, you have to pray."

It wasn't worth a fuss. Especially one that Mom would hear about first thing in the morning. I sat on the side of the bed and pretended to close my eyes.

Miranda, off the bed and on her knees with her hands folded, went first, "Dear God," she said, "Thank you for putting Aunt Mof in Mikey's room. Bring Mommy and Daddy home soon, and can we please have pizza again tomorrow." She wasn't kidding. I looked.

Stacy was speaking after the last pause, picking up where Miranda left off. "And thank you for Mikey, and please let him get a check mark and a smiley face on the most important test of his life. Amen."

Later, sprawled out on the sofa after a hot shower, I couldn't help thinking how long it had been since Mom had prayed with me at bedtime.

Sometimes I really missed those days. "God, help me," I whispered. "How can I call myself a Christian and be part of this . . . this . . . mess?"

Long after I heard Mom and Dad come in, I lay awake thinking. The CD player was silent, and the TV was dark. I was a Christian, wasn't I? I remembered that Sunday three years ago when I'd confessed my sin and repented. It was real. So why was I acting like it hadn't happened?

Thursday morning, Mrs. Valbueno was on time for a change, but she had left her usual cheerful face at home. I took my history book and notebook out of my backpack and was shoving the backpack under the desk when I started sensing an unusual mood in the room. I paused, trying not to turn my head, and cut my eyes over to first Carlos and then Scott. They must have already noticed it; they were sitting like statues, staring at the blank chalkboard. I must have missed something. She sure looks sour, I thought, glancing around. Everyone seemed to feel it. I sat looking at Mrs. Valbueno and wondered who had ruffled her feathers. With her eyebrows drawn close together and her head tipped back a little so that her lips sort of pinched together, she picked up her roll book and started taking attendance.

She called seven or eight names before she paused. "Scott Cunningham." She said his name in a slow, deliberate tone and looked at him for several long seconds. I held my breath. So, that was it. Suddenly the whole situation was clear. She—and probably Mr. Fielder—were pretty sure that Scott had taken the test, but they couldn't prove it. At least they weren't going to do anything about it right then. Everyone who knew us would know that if Scott was involved, then Carlos and I were involved.

Scott shifted in his seat, looking embarrassed and probably seeing the situation as clearly as I did. Carlos and I got much the same treatment when our names were called. Carlos's dark face flushed a deep pink. The hour seemed endless. I deliberately kept my attention on my book, or on the chalkboard, avoiding eye contact with Mrs. Valbueno or anyone else.

"If looks could kill," Carlos whispered breathlessly when we met at our lockers after class. He fumbled with the wrapper on a peppermint.

"I died in there," Scott said. He leaned his forehead against the cold metal locker.

"They know," I said, speaking almost to myself. "But they aren't doing anything about it."

"What can they do?" Scott asked hopefully. His eyes glistened a little as he spoke. "They already asked me, and I answered."

"Yeah, well, you know it's not over. And you never actually said you didn't take the thing. And anyhow, they're going to get around to cross-examining Carlos and me soon enough. And I just might confess and get it over with!"

Carlos and Scott looked at me. I knew what they were thinking. If I did confess—and I sure didn't want to—then the final tennis tournament of the season might make very sad history. There were other good players on the team, but we carried the load.

"Just wait, Prickett," Scott pleaded. "Let's give it some time and see what happens."

It occurred to me that nowhere in the Bible does it say to "wait and see what happens."

I found that it didn't take long to see what was happening. I had always looked forward to fourth period—math—because it was the only other class I shared with Amber and because I was good at math and could sometimes show off a little. But showing off was the last thing on my mind in class that Thursday. I only wanted the whole problem to go away. I really needed to talk to Dad.

"Hey, Mike," Nathan said very quietly. He leaned up close from the desk behind me. "Maybe I could come over one night this week and we could study. You know. History."

I took a sharp breath, instantly aware that Nathan was asking me to share the stolen exam with him. "I have the same review sheet you have," I mouthed almost silently with my head turned slightly and with my lips kind of stretched over sideways toward Nathan's ear. Suddenly it was clear as glass that my reputation as a Christian wasn't worth a hill of beans right now.

I looked around the room wondering how many others saw me like Nathan did. He'd never been to my house, and we had less than nothing in common. If I went to the kind of places Nathan went to, I could expect to be grounded for life. Suddenly, in my mind I could hear Dad repeat for the millionth time, "Birds of a feather flock together." Was I in the flock with Nathan Saladin? Never. At least I never had been before.

Nathan continued to whisper for a few moments, but I wasn't listening. I wasn't thinking clearly either. I almost failed a pop quiz in math that would normally have been another ace.

Scott was waiting at the lockers after what seemed an eternity in fourth period. "You'll never guess who wants to study with us," Scott said as I joined him.

I didn't care, and I didn't answer. I wasn't up to guessing.

"Smith and Anderson," Scott said, as though I were eager to hear it.

More in our same flock of featherless birdbrains, I thought, heaving a hard sigh.

"Mike," Scott mumbled. He looked down at his shoes, but sort of motioned down the hall with his left shoulder. I looked in the direction he was gesturing, trying not to turn my head. Amber was walking our way, and for once, she was alone. Without meaning to, I found myself standing taller, lifting my head a little, and taking kind of a casual position up against the wall of lockers. I had waited a long time for a moment alone with Amber, and here she came. Scott occupied himself with organizing his locker, while pretending to ignore me for a few moments.

"Hey Amber." I tried to sound friendly and casual without being too bold and direct. I was sharply aware of my tone of voice—a little too high—and how I had my feet placed—one flat on the floor and one flat behind me up against my locker with my knee bent. My science book was balanced on my knee, and my right hand rested on top of it, to keep it from hitting the floor. I hoped I looked more cool, composed, and collected than I felt.

Catching my eye for only a moment, Amber looked away. She didn't have to say it. I knew what she was thinking.

"Come on," Scott said, with an awkward whack on my back.

Later I collected quarters from Scott and Carlos and walked toward the cafeteria to get our drinks, while they got our lunch sacks and took the shortcut to the courtyard to find a bench.

Passing the foyer near the front offices, I couldn't help walking over to take another look at the trophy case. We had all stood here many times, admiring the gold and feeling the school pride that was shared by almost everyone at Cross Springs High School. The display was in a huge wooden and glass frame, and it held memories going back forty years. The peculiar smell of the wood brought to mind the thousands of hands that had rested on its surface during the years it had been there. At least fifty basketball awards, plaques, and other trophies filled the case. The thing that made the tennis trophies even more special is that Cross Springs had never lost a district tournament. The trophy for every year—going back seventeen years—stood lined up in the case in the front hallway. The tennis team felt colossal pressure to succeed, but we were also very confident.

A hand rested lightly on my shoulder, startling me. "Uh, Mr. Fielder," I stammered. My mind drew a blank, and I stood there several moments looking like an imbecile and feeling trapped by his hand on my shoulder. Shuffling my feet a little, I managed to turn and get a quick sideways glance at his expression. Disappointment was written all over his face. I felt like confessing all I had done. I wanted to confess. I needed to confess. But, there was Scott and Carlos to consider. And there was the tournament to think about. We would probably be expelled. After several very long seconds I felt a light squeeze on my shoulder. Mr. Fielder walked away.

Feeling lightheaded and totally baffled, I stood staring at the trophy case. All at once I knew what was happening. Clear as glass, I knew. I looked down the hall at Mr. Fielder's retreating figure, and then back at the past years of tennis trophies. Because these trophies were very important to the school, and because

Coach and Mr. Fielder, and probably others, wanted to continue an unbroken tradition, they were going to wait until after tomorrow's tournament to let the axe fall on those involved in the theft. Somehow I knew that Dad would never wait like that.

Well, maybe I'd just unburden myself right now and see what happened. I couldn't take the pressure much longer anyhow. And besides, I hadn't taken that test—I'd only tried to return it.

I couldn't help noticing the slight change in tone and conversation at the teachers' lunch table when I passed by on the way to the drink machine. I could feel a dozen pair of eyes boring in on me.

I shot a quarter into the machine and got my soda. I deliberately looked at the teacher's lunch table as I got drinks for Scott and Carlos. *You want another trophy?* I shouted silently. *You got it!* I was trembling inside.

By the time we made it to practice that afternoon, I had calmed down and was beginning to focus on the coming tournament. Alpharetta was an hour and a half drive away, so the bus would probably leave right after first period tomorrow. I'd have given a new pair of tennis shoes to leave *before* first period.

"Mike, Scott, use the north court. Dan, Kyle, south. Carlos, you'll have to fill in doubles with Mark. Work his backhand." Coach walked off, unwrapping another stick of gum as he directed other players where to work out and what strokes to emphasize.

I didn't have to look at Carlos to know he was disappointed in his assignment. He was a good player, but he didn't care much for doubles, and he didn't care much for sharing a court with Mark. But he'd deal with it.

"Let's go." Carlos spoke in Mark's general direction as he straightened his drooping shoulders and brushed wisps of hair from his face.

Warm-up usually lasted half an hour, with plenty of quick steps and powerful volleys. Scott's backhand was almost more fierce than his forehand, leading me to aim most of my shots to his right side. My backhand was controlled and strong, but never totally dependable. I could count on three out of four backhand shots when Scott stood across my net. We worked out almost forty-five minutes before Coach called "game." Then, for the next two hours we played game, set, and match. And for two hours Coach walked from court to court, commenting, suggesting, demonstrating, and encouraging. I was focused. I was ready.

Chapter 5

Stacy and Miranda had the driveway covered with bikes and toys when I crossed the yard. "Better get that mess put away before Dad comes in," I said. They ignored me, and I hurried to the kitchen, hoping for a snack. The place smelled like cookies, but none were in sight, and Mom's favorite hiding places were empty. I knew better than to ask, so I searched a few minutes longer before giving up. "Probably took 'em to the neighbors." I poured a glass of milk instead.

I could hear Mom and Aunt Mof laughing and talking back in my room as I headed that way. For sisters, they were really different. Mom always seemed so calm and serious, and Aunt Mof, well . . . maybe it was partly her red hair and loud laughing voice, but she seemed somehow more fun. Right now, though, it was Mom whoopin' it up.

"And do you remember the look on Pastor Malone's face," she said, hardly able to talk for laughing, "when we hid all the light bulbs in the speaker's cottage at summer camp that first year?"

"Too bad he didn't find out about it before dark," Aunt Mof added, giggling like a little girl. "Ahhh, he was a good sport, though."

"Oops," Mom said, pretending to be mortified when she saw me standing in the doorway. They both laughed again. Mom placed a few more sugar stars on a tray of brownies and turned sideways to squeeze the tray and herself past me.

"Ready to work?" Aunt Mof asked. She adjusted the reading glasses that held her unruly hair back from her face.

"Work?"

"History!"

"Oh . . . uh . . . I guess," I answered, wishing I hadn't come in the room.

I hadn't noticed before, but her whole bed seemed covered with index cards. There were hundreds of them. Aunt Mof was drawing them into a pile and stacking them up. When she finished, the cards must have been over four inches high.

Seeing the blank look on my face, Aunt Mof picked up the pages of history review questions and waved them at the stack of cards.

"Ahhh . . . " I mumbled, not yet convinced that she expected me to absorb the questions and answers from that mountain of cards.

"You know, Michael," she said, "this is a project that I'm sure you can't do alone."

So, what else is new? I thought.

She went on, "But we both know that with God all things are possible. Right?"

I just nodded, hating to show how skeptical I really felt.

"And remember that verse in Second Timothy: *Study to shew thyself approved unto God, a workman that needeth not to be ashamed, rightly dividing the word of truth.*"

She waited until I nodded again. "We know that God says to study, right? So we can be sure that it's pleasing to God when we ask for help in something He's already told us to do."

Without waiting for me to nod, or answer, she bowed her head and asked God to help me concentrate and learn every one of the four hundred and nine answers on the cards she had written out. It was a short prayer that left me feeling somehow encouraged.

"Sit, sit." Aunt Mof waved toward my desk chair.

I sat, hiking a well-worn sneaker up over my left knee and slowly shaking my head at the huge stack of study cards.

She smiled and held up a card. “Does *one* card look easier?”

I shrugged and uncrossed my legs.

“Of course you can—and will—easily learn this one card. Then you’ll learn one more,” she said as she held up another, “and one more.”

She looked at the first card and read out a question. “Who was the builder of the first world empire?

“Uhhh . . .” I paused, familiar with the question but not the answer.

“Nimrod.” She said the answer before three seconds had passed. I might have thought of it.

“In what year did Rome fall?”

“Well . . .” I said, settling back against the chair.

“A.D. 500,” she answered.

“What event should be associated with the date A.D. 1000?”

I just shrugged.

“The Crusades.”

“Who was the builder of the first world empire?”

“Nimrod?” I guessed, thinking I had just heard that one.

She nodded, putting that card in a separate stack. A very short stack.

“In what year did Rome fall?

I knew she had just asked that one, but I hesitated a moment too long.

“A.D. 500,” she said.

I knew it. Another couple of seconds and I’d have spit it out.

“What event should be associated with the date A.D. 1000?”

“The Crusades?”

Aunt Mof lowered her cards and looked at me with her head sort of tilted and her face lit up. “Are you asking, or telling?”

“Uh . . . well . . . I’m telling. The Crusades.”

“Good,” she said firmly, placing the Crusades card on the short stack and lifting her cards to read the next one.

She read quickly, giving me only about three seconds on each card. If I hesitated too long, she’d give the answer, and I’d hear the question again after a couple of cards. When I had ten cards on the short stack, she picked them up and asked all ten again. This was going fast. From the first question to the review of the first ten took only about five minutes. Aunt Mof was energetic and fun. She could even make study a sport. Well, sort of.

I was reviewing my fourth stack of ten when I saw Aunt Mof look toward the door and wave Scott and Carlos to chairs. Then without a pause, she directed the next questions to them.

“Who became the military governor of Japan after World War II?”

Both of them sat there like dummies with their mouths open.

“General Douglas MacArthur. What is referred to as ‘China’s Sorrow’?”

“As what?”

“The Yellow River. Scott, who became the military governor of Japan after World War II?”

“MacArthur?” Scott asked, not sounding sure at all.

“Are you asking me?” Aunt Mof said playfully in an exaggerated tone.

I couldn’t help flashing a smile.

“General Douglas MacArthur,” Scott said, sounding more convinced.

When Mom called supper, I was surprised to see that an hour had flown by. For the first time in weeks I was feeling a little encouraged about the history exam. I had a long, long way to go, but I was on my way.

I woke up Friday morning to the smell of breakfast. For as long as I'd been playing tennis, Mom fixed a huge breakfast on competition days. It was almost a tradition at our house.

"You're up early." Mom turned from the stove as I staggered to the kitchen door.

I took a deep breath. The aroma of bacon had lured me to the kitchen.

"I think I'll compete every day," I said.

Dad joined me at the table about twenty minutes later. "Ahhh, tournament day," he said, diving into bacon, eggs, and biscuits. "You should compete more often," he added, giving me a punch on the shoulder. "No more trophies, though." He winked. "The house is getting all cluttered up with those big gaudy things."

I just smiled. I knew Dad was extremely proud of my tennis trophies. Once I heard him explaining the history of every award to a neighbor in such detail that I was embarrassed and sort of felt sorry for the neighbor who had to endure the report.

"Uh, Mike," Dad said, and his tone of voice immediately caught my attention. "I won't be able to make it to this tournament. I hate it, but . . . it's unavoidable. Business from out of town. But I'll be praying for you."

I was sure the business really was important. Dad had never missed one of my competitions. I was disappointed, but actually I hardly knew they were there on tournament days. The schedule was so hectic, and the focus so intense that the team seemed to exist in another world from the time we left school until we got home.

"Your mother will be there, of course."

"Wouldn't miss it." Mom laid her hand on my shoulder for a moment.

Dad finished and left for work. I took my last bite and then put my plate in the sink.

"Mike," Mom said . . . and then hesitated. "You know I pray for you every day . . . sometimes every hour," she said.

Then she took my face in both her hands and said, “Mike, always keep your heart and mind pure before God.”

I nodded and reached for my tennis racket and gym bag. “Sure,” I mumbled.

“I’ll see you in Alpharetta.” She waved as I bounded out the back door.

Keep my heart and mind pure? Too late, I thought, thinking of the stolen exam and the mess we were in. She must know something. But if she knows, why didn’t she ask about it? I couldn’t help thinking of the Bible verse in Proverbs, *The wicked flee when no man pursueth*. I was guilty for sure . . . but wicked? I couldn’t let myself think about it.

Minutes after the bell set off our escape from incarceration in history class, the boys varsity squad began gathering in the gym locker room. The locker room smelled like sweaty towels and new tennis shoes. It always smelled like sweaty towels and new tennis shoes. It was a familiar odor that I was comfortable with. I was relieved to be included in the usual joking and friendly hubbub. I guess I’d been sort of apprehensive about how we’d be accepted in the group after the cold shoulder we’d suffered in several classes. Rejection on the team would have meant a major problem with concentration, and almost certain failure.

“Hey, Mike,” Arnie shouted, “you got room in your house for another trophy?”

“Always room for one more,” I bantered back.

“Bus is ready.” Coach waved us out of the locker room. The contrast between his white socks and his dingy shoes was glaring. He walked toward the bus, his pockets bulging with tennis balls and packs of chewing gum.

Carrying gym bags and rackets, we drifted toward the waiting bus and got in line behind the girls varsity team. We wouldn’t see much of the girls once we were in Alpharetta, but they’d make the trip there and back more fun.

The bus was only half full with nine guys, six girls, Coach, Miss Reynolds—the girls' coach—and two parents. But with gym bags littering the aisle and tennis shoes and bare knees sticking out here and there, the bus seemed packed. Everyone had a grip on his tennis racket. We held them like security blankets. My graphite racket with its oversized head sure looked different from the old wooden racket Dad used to play with.

We spent most of the drive wondering out loud about the draw and comparing the possibilities to the seeding chart from last year. Even Coach hadn't seen the schedule yet. We were all familiar with the umpires and had our favorites. There were a few umpires we hoped were off the planet for the weekend.

After almost an hour and a half of nonstop talk and good natured heckling, the bus pulled into the Alpharetta High School parking lot. We followed the girls off the bus and waited for Coach to lead the way.

He headed for the office. "Hang around the bus till I get the schedule."

We were only an hour and a half north of Cross Springs, but the air here seemed almost five degrees cooler. The prickle of excitement on tournament days was like a chill down the spine.

We'd be playing teams from six schools. Most of them had already arrived and were milling around the area. Parents were setting up lawn chairs, and here and there a few coolers with cold drinks were opening up. I didn't see Mom, but I didn't expect her until later, since she usually came with Scott's mom. Carlos's grandmother didn't drive and seldom left home. A few minutes later Coach handed Miss Reynolds her schedule sheet, and she and the girls started walking toward the Middle School where their games were being held.

"Okay, listen up guys," Coach called. "Carlos and Mark, 11 o'clock, court four, doubles against Marietta. Uhhh . . . let's see . . . their guys are Sonny Tressler and Brandon Smith. You have half an hour."

I knew Carlos wasn't too happy about having to play doubles, but Mark's partner was down with the flu, and at least one doubles team was required for the competition this year.

"Arnie, 11 o'clock, court six. You tangle with David Black from Stone Mountain. Scott, uhhh . . . 11 o'clock, court one. Covington. You play Alan Armada."

Coach glanced up to gesture Carlos, Mark, Arnie, and Scott to get going.

"Okay, . . . " Coach studied the schedule. "Dan, 1 P.M., court nine. You whip Bret McCollum from Augusta. Kyle, 1 P.M., court four, Tony Simonds from Forsyth. Dustin, 1 P.M. Matt Houston from Decatur. Jacob, 1 P.M. You'll play Larry Pruehsner from Covington.

With a nod, Coach dismissed the one o'clock group and I stood there alone, wishing I'd been called with the 11 o'clock group.

"Mike, hmmm . . . You play at 3 P.M. . . . Let's see . . . uh . . . oh yeah, court two, Derek Gardner from Macon." Coach took masking tape and attached the schedule to the door of the bus. I had a lot of time to kill, and I'd spend it at the sidelines of other games. I walked off thinking, Derek Gardner . . . Derek Gardner . . . I thought I knew the name. He was the guy who had taken the game from Scott last year. Cross Springs won the trophy, but it was close. If every other player hadn't done as well as they did, it would have broken our sixteen-year record. I knew for sure that Scott would remember the name too. Because of Derek, Scott had been the only player on the team last year without a trophy.

Before 11:00, Carlos and Mark were on court four with Sonny and Brandon, hitting a few back and forth. The umpire, a new guy we hadn't seen before, was going from court to court talking to each set of players for a minute or two. When he walked off, they were free to start the match. After a spin of the racket, Carlos started the game with the first serve. It was powerful, slamming hard into the net. Fault. His next serve was less powerful, but made its mark. One thing about Carlos's serve, if his first one made it into the service court, it was seldom returned. However, it seldom made it in the first time. I watched for fifteen minutes or so, mesmerized by the action, the muscles in my arms flinching involuntarily with each powerful return.

When Sonny started to serve, I drifted toward court one to see how Scott was doing against Alan. I sat on a bench nearby just in time to hear Alan say, “Advantage in.” Then he tossed the ball for what would be his last serve of the first game. Scott couldn’t return it.

“Game,” the umpire called. I hadn’t seen an umpire during Carlos and Mark’s first game. Scott and Alan switched sides, and Scott prepared to serve. About that time, I saw Mom drive by. I headed over to the parking lot, hanging back a little, hoping no one would see me with the pink eyesore. I met her and Mrs. Cunningham walking across the parking lot, and I took their lawn chairs from them.

“Over here,” I said, and then set up the chairs and a small cooler with their iced tea far enough from the court that Scott wouldn’t be distracted.

I spent the rest of the morning drifting from court one to court four. From time to time I’d stand watching one of our other guys. It was a mentally exhausting time, and I hadn’t begun to focus on my own game yet. I’d much rather have had the 11:00 A.M. time slot to pour all my morning energies into the game. By 1 P.M., the first set of matches was over. Scott won his match 6-4, 4-6 and 6-2. After twenty-eight games he was ready to sit in the shade for the rest of the day. Carlos and Mark lost the doubles match 6-3, 6-4. It was a major disappointment. I felt sorry for both of them. Arnie won his match against Stone Mountain. While Dan and Kyle and Dustin got started on their matches, Carlos and Scott and I made our way to the lunch tent.

By 1:30 we were on our way to the middle school to see how the girls were doing. We watched Miss Reynolds flit from court to court where she watched, nodded, and made suggestions. So far the girls had won three, and three other matches were in progress.

We watched a while, and I found myself wishing that Amber played.

By 2:30 we headed back to the high school to check on the games in progress. Dan and Kyle were finished and had won their matches. Dustin was in the last five minutes of a match that he lost. It was a big loss, and it put super pressure on me. If I lost my match, then Cross Springs would not see that eighteenth trophy this year. I began to mentally focus on the next couple of hours. Scott and Carlos went for cold drinks, and I sat in one of the lawn chairs that Mom and Mrs. Cunningham had left when they went into town for lunch.

Derek walked onto the court a few minutes before three o'clock, and I picked up my gym bag and took out a new can of balls. Pulling back the seal, hearing the whoosh of air, and smelling the new rubber smell always stimulated my senses and helped me prepare for a match. Yes. I was ready. The umpire came onto the court and directed the spin of the racket. It would be my serve first. I considered that to be my mental advantage.

Standing to the right of the center back service line, I closed my eyes, deliberately focused my full attention on the moment and stood motionless for several seconds before tossing the ball high and straight up. I came down on it hard, sending the ball to the inside corner of Derek's service court. Perfect shot. Derek didn't flinch until after it was too late. 15–love. I stepped to the left of the center service line as Derek moved to his receiving stance. After a moment's pause to concentrate, I sent my serve like a shot fired into the net. My second serve was more controlled and much softer and was returned instantly, but a little awkwardly, I thought. I easily lobbed it to the far corner out of Derek's reach. 30–love. I began to feel more relaxed. This wasn't the Derek Gardner I remembered from last year. I quickly took my place and sent a hard serve over the net and directly toward Derek's waiting racket. He was slow on the return and sent it to the net. 40–love.

I couldn't help wondering what the trophy looked like this year. I stood to the left of the service line, tossed the ball, and sent it like a bullet just outside Derek's service court. The next serve was more controlled, softer and apparently a bit overconfident. Double fault. 40–15. I wouldn't let that happen again. After one more powerful first serve, and one more momentary delay by Derek, I had the final point and the game.

I glanced over at Scott. He was watching intently, but not with the glow of admiration that I expected. Derek and I met at the net and made the customary side switch. Suddenly, I saw Derek in a whole new light. My brain must have been in a holding pattern not to have realized what Derek's problem was. The sun. It was just past 3 P.M. and the sun was blinding on the east end of the court.

Standing far back from the service court, I waited for Derek's first serve. I was still waiting when I heard it whistle past me. Talk about humiliating. 15–love. Stepping over to the left service court, I moved my head back and forth looking for a spot where I might be able to avoid the direct sun. Pinching my eyes mostly shut, I bent my knees more than usual and more than necessary and lowered my head, looking for a way to clearly see Derek's serve. I heard the ball go by. "Outside," I heard the line judge say.

Good, I thought. This was terrible. At least Derek had managed to return most of mine.

His next serve was much softer, and I returned it deep into his court. We managed a short rally before Derek hit the ball outside the baseline. 15–15.

That's better, I breathed silently. I was unable to return Derek's next serve. 30–15. Then I returned the following serve hard into the net. 40–15. His final serve of the second game was as humiliating for me as his first serve. Game.

We started game three with one win apiece. After game three, which I lost with a deceptive show of good sportsmanship, I was more than glad to switch back to the west end of the court. For the next two sets, as we switched sides after every odd-numbered game, the winner of almost every game was determined by who was facing the sun. I was emotionally exhausted and physically tired. My focus was drifting and my feet dragging. Thankfully, the sun was also drifting, and it was becoming possible to play a defensive game again. Still a challenge, but quite possible.

"Murder, isn't it?" Derek said as we stood near the net post for a drink and a brief rest.

"Yeah," I agreed. With one set each, we were both feeling the strain of the past hour and a half.

Walking back to prepare for my first serve of the third set, I noticed Mom sitting several yards back of the fence. I hadn't noticed her during all the previous games, and it bothered me some that I noticed her now. I was sharply aware that my focus and concentration were slipping.

Standing at the service line with my eyes closed, I breathed deeply, drew my thoughts together and waited. *I wish Dad could have come.* The thought flashed across my mind. *Stop it.* I screamed at myself. *Focus.*

Derek was poised and ready, slowly moving up and down on the balls of his feet, with his knees bent, and his racket ready for either a forehand or backhand swing. I stood, berating myself and working on my focus for so long that I suddenly noticed Derek stand tall and drop his racket to his side. I nodded at him and watched him snap back in ready position as I tossed the ball. Coming down with fury, I sent the ball to the inside edge of Derek's service court. Perfect shot. With precision and power Derek took a strong forehand swing and sent the ball deep into my court. I was sure it was going to be outside and I froze. It was on the line. Love–15.

Get it together, Mike, I shouted at myself. My concentration was choking up. Moving to the left of the service line, I drew on every ounce of mental power I could muster. My serve was good, and Derek sent a high lob back over the net as I quickly positioned myself under the falling ball. With perfect timing I landed a mighty overhead smash that sent the ball blasting into Derek's court just inches above the net.

As the line judge retrieved the ball, I worked hard to keep a huge grin of success off my face. 15–15. My third serve produced a fairly long rally that ended in my last return skittering along the top of the net for several inches before it fell, rolling into Derek's court. 30–15. I was breathing hard as I collected myself for the next serve. I tossed the ball high and came down hard. Net fault. I tossed again and once again hit the net. Double fault. 30–30. It was seeming like a long, long day. I was wishing again that I had drawn an early game—maybe 11 A.M., like Scott. I'd be sitting on the sidelines in a lawn chair with a cold drink.

STOP IT, I screamed at myself. Once a player's concentration begins to choke up, it's really hard—often impossible—to effectively focus again.

"*Lord*," I prayed silently, with my eyes closed in a position of gathering concentration, "*please help me focus*." But I wasn't sure God was listening to my prayers right now.

The first game of the third set fell to me, but Derek took the next two games. After another forty-five minutes we stood at four games each in the third set. My legs were rubbery. My mind was rubbery. I noticed that Derek didn't seem in much better shape. Every serve and every return was an overwhelming effort, and I couldn't shake the feeling that if my mind could stay centered, then my feet and hands would cooperate.

By this time, ours was the last game in progress and those who hadn't left were silently gathered along the four sides of our court. Only after an especially good shot—or an especially dumb one—would there be the sound of OOOOOhs . . . or Ahhhhhhs.

The umpire stepped in before we switched sides and called a fifteen-minute rest. I was almost afraid that if I sat down I wouldn't be able to get up, but I was grateful for the break.

Coach brought me water and gave instructions for ten minutes straight, hardly taking a breath. He gripped his racket and demonstrated, and reminded, and encouraged while I focused on the fact that Mom and Dad were praying for me.

After almost fifteen minutes I was standing to my feet when a Bible verse I'd learned years ago popped into my mind: *He giveth power to the faint; and to them that have no might he increaseth strength.* It came from somewhere in Isaiah or maybe Psalms, and I was startled by how clearly it rang in my mind. I took a deep breath and turned back to the game.

Derek stood behind his service line with his eyes closed while I slowly moved up and down on the balls of my feet, flexing my arms and hands, prepared for whatever he delivered.

Wham. I caught Derek's first serve and lobbed it high over his head, sending it within inches of the base line. Love–15. Stepping to the left side of the court, I bent my knees and hunched down a little, waiting for his next serve. It whistled past me. "Outside," the line judge called. His second try was also a whistler, but it was clearly inside the line. Expecting a softer second serve, I wasn't prepared, and I let it get away from me.

"*Concentrate*," I muttered. 15–15. Derek's next serve led to a rally that seemed to go on and on. There was nowhere I could send the ball that he couldn't return it. The pressure was relentless. Eventually the line judge called "outside," and Derek called the score 15–30. I was on top again, but just for a moment. I missed his next serve and heard Derek call 30–30. Returning his next serve high over his head, I watched as Derek sprinted backward, caught the ball with the neck of his racket, and sent it into the crowd. I heard a low murmur of "Ahhhhhh . . . ," as those rooting for Derek felt his disappointment. 30–40.

I wasn't even in the receiving stance yet when I saw another serve on its way over the net. I made a dive for it, caught the ball with the tip of my racket, and then watched the ball touch the net as it fell into Derek's court. Derek's jaw jutted out and clinched tightly shut before I saw, rather than heard him say, "game." One more game for Cross Springs High School and the eighteenth trophy would be ours.

My serve. *He giveth power to the faint; and to them that have no might he increaseth strength.* I took several deep breaths and looked intently at the spot in Derek's court where I intended to place the ball. I consciously relaxed my shoulder muscles, and then my stomach muscles. *Deliberately and with power*. I tossed the ball, waited for the perfect moment, and then came down with a powerful slam. Derek returned the ball with a high lob up over my head. I took four or five quick steps backwards and was waiting with my racket in the backhand position when the ball bounced. *Wham*—it cleared the net without an inch to spare. Derek was right there to catch the volley and drive it to the edge of the service line.

"Good shot," I said. Derek nodded. Love–15. A short rally ending in a net ball for Derek followed the next serve. 15–15. It was taking me longer and longer to focus and gather my thoughts. My mind was drifting, and my legs felt weak. "Foot fault," the umpire called, when I delivered an otherwise strong serve. I tried again. My soft serve landed just inside the back service line, and Derek put it away with an effective drive. 15–30.

Focus, Mike, focus. Taking a chance, I rushed the net and managed to catch Derek's return and drive it to the sideline up close to the net. Perfect. I doubted that that would work again. 30–30. Tipping the net on the following serve, I called "let," and tossed for another try. Good delivery, and strong return. I sent the ball back to the far right corner and was surprised to see it coming back again. Sending it to the far left corner, it met Derek there too. His control was outstanding as he carefully sent a soft, short lob just over the net and out of my reach.

"Nice one," I forced myself to say. 30–40. *He giveth power to the faint; and to them that have no might he increaseth strength.* Tossing high, I directed all my physical and emotional energy into my swing as I drove the serve into Derek's court. Derek never touched the ball. Deuce. My next serve was a little sloppy, but Derek drove it into the net. Advantage in. One more point and it could all be over. Stepping to the opposite service side, I paused a long time to focus my full attention on the spot I was aiming for. Derek hunched down and kept moving, ready for whatever I delivered.

Relax and take a deep breath, I instructed myself. I shook first one hand, then took the racket in that hand to shake the other. Then I tossed, and I came down hard at the exact spot I was aiming for. Derek sent the ball back just inside the base line. I was waiting for it and sent a solid return to the far left corner of Derek's court, forcing him to display incredible speed and agility. Even I was impressed. He managed to send the ball just barely over the net, but I was waiting there, and I drove it with all the strength I had left in me to the far right corner of the court. No one could have reached that ball.

It was over. Cross Springs would keep an unbroken record. I couldn't move for several moments. When Derek met me at the net for the customary handshake, I was in a daze, physically and emotionally exhausted.

The subdued crowd suddenly became enthusiastically loud and excited. I endured fierce hugs and pounding pats of congratulations. Carlos and Scott were all smiles and kept jabbing their fists in the air. Coach was pounding me black and blue with affectionate punches and whacks on the back. Within moments the adrenaline kicked in and I was bouncing around with the rest of the team. It didn't take long for Derek and his group of players and parents from Macon to drift toward the parking lot. I couldn't help feeling a momentary stab of compassion for Derek. He had put as much into the game as I had.

I spotted Mom standing alone next to her two lawn chairs, and I hurried over.

"Congratulations," she said, wrapping her arms around me. There were tears in her eyes.

"Want a ride home?" she asked, waving toward the parking lot.

"Uh, well . . . maybe I should stick with the rest of the team," I said. Mom gave me another quick hug before we were joined by Scott's mother.

Coach caught my attention when he motioned us over to the judges' pavilion for our trophies. Many of the players from other schools had already been awarded their prizes and left. Without too much hoopla, the individual winners were handed trophies, and Coach was given trophy number eighteen for the display case in the front hall. His smile was as bright as the gold trophy.

The team wandered slowly toward the bus, talking and laughing with the energizer of victory. The girls boarded the bus first, and the guys hung around outside holding rackets, gym bags and trophies.

What happened next is still a blur in my mind—a painful memory. Arnie and Kyle climbed onto the bus, and I stepped in behind them. Just as I put my full weight on the first step, moving toward the second, the attached edge of the step came off and sent me stumbling to the ground, forcing Carlos to his knees in the grass and almost knocking Scott over. I instinctively gripped my trophy to my chest and dropped my racket and gym bag. It all happened fast—the racket must have landed under my feet, keeping me from catching myself. My knees—both knees—scraped hard on the sloping edge of the cement curb. I jumped up instantly, suffering severe embarrassment and very bloody knees. I wasn't aware of the bloody knees for several seconds, my humiliation was so sharp.

Waving off help and sympathy, I hurried up over the broken step and down the aisle to a seat on the bus. I fumbled around in my gym bag for my sweaty towel and started to blot up the blood, when one of the girls—Stephanie—reached over and handed me her clean one instead. At that moment I couldn't decide whether I was thrilled with her attention or further humiliated by it. Several moments later Coach came down the aisle, took one look, and left the bus. Carlos moved out of his seat so Stephanie could sit down next to me, and after a few moments, attention drifted away from me, and on to more interesting subjects. Coach boarded the bus again, tossed me the first-aid kit, a towel, and a couple of ice bags.

"Mmmm . . . that must hurt really bad," Stephanie breathed with a moan.

"Oh, not really." I put on a brave front. I cleaned up my knees, and Stephanie squirted on some first-aid spray. Then she stood hesitantly.

"Thanks for the help," I said, trying to sound casual and wishing she would stay. I watched her walk to the front of the bus and join the other girls.

"That's rough," Scott said, sliding into the seat that Stephanie just left.

"Stupid and clumsy," I mumbled.

"Nah . . . I saw that step break off."

"Still stupid and clumsy," I said under my breath.

"Hurt a lot?" Scott went on.

"What d'you think?" I said, and right away I was sorry. Actually, it did hurt a lot, and it made it worse to have to pretend that it didn't.

I noticed Coach looking back at us, when suddenly a terrible thought filled my mind. If Mr. Fielder had been waiting until after the tournament to call the three of us in for a little talk . . . well . . . the tournament was over. I couldn't help wondering if even Coach might confront us. My chest tightened and a heaviness seemed to drift over me, but Coach stayed at the front of the bus. Of course I couldn't be sure, but if Coach was deliberately avoiding the confrontation, then in a way, he was almost as guilty of the cover-up as we were. I hoped it wasn't so.

Chapter 6

I limped through the back door and stood in the kitchen a moment. Ahhh, my favorite perfume—pizza. There were several boxes on the table. Mom's and Dad's cars were both in the driveway, so I guessed Mom got in too late from the tournament to cook. Fine with me. I saw the twins absorbed in some kids' show on TV as I made my way painfully back to my room, looking for the rest of the family.

"So, I'll start the job in Cleveland in about six weeks," Dad was saying.

"You're going to Cleveland?" I gasped, hardly believing what I was hearing.

"Michael, you're home!" I had clearly taken him by surprise.

"You're going to Cleveland?" I repeated.

"Well, Michael," Dad said, "I'm sorry you heard it like this. I had planned to talk to you alone."

"You're going to Cleveland?" I said again, not yet making sense of what I had heard.

"We're *all* going to Cleveland," Dad said.

"What?" I was feeling more confused by the moment.

"Come sit down, dear," Mom said, patting the side of the bed. When she called me "Dear," it usually came before something I didn't want to hear. And I definitely didn't want to hear about moving to Cleveland.

"Congratulations," Aunt Mof said in a tone much less enthusiastic than her usual lively voice. She reached for the trophy that I held gripped in both hands. I stared at her a moment before I realized what she was talking about, and then I handed over the prize. Suddenly I noticed that Aunt Mof was sitting in the wheelchair. It was the first time in the four days she had been here that I'd seen her out of bed.

I stared at the wheelchair for a moment before snapping my attention back to Dad.

My throat constricted so tightly that I could hardly breathe. "I can't leave here," I said in a pathetic, pleading voice.

"Michael," Mom cried out, causing all of us to turn suddenly toward her. "Your knees." She leaned down to examine my wounds. I had forgotten all about my knees during the last few minutes, but now that she brought them to my attention, they immediately started throbbing again.

"I just fell getting on the bus. Why do we have to go to Cleveland?"

"Okay," Dad said, heaving a sigh and gesturing to the chair in front of my computer. I walked over and paced around next to it.

"Remember last Wednesday when your mom and I were out late at a business meeting?"

I remembered. And I remembered the momentary look that had crossed Aunt Mof's face when she mentioned the meeting.

"Yeah," I said.

Dad paused, looking at me.

"Yes, sir."

"Well, we've been exploring the possibility of opening another consulting business in Cleveland because, as you've no doubt gathered from discussions you've overheard, work is very slow around here. Frank will stay here and manage this office."

Frank is Dad's office assistant, and a good friend, and it was true that Mom and Dad seemed to always be talking about Dad's lack of business.

"Why Cleveland?" I asked. I was beginning to feel weak.

"We're familiar with Cleveland. Your Mom grew up there, and Martha," Dad waved in Aunt Mof's direction, "has a lot of contacts there. And the economy is strong in Cleveland."

I sat down.

"I think you'll like Cleveland." Aunt Mof hugged my trophy and spoke with a sad smile.

I couldn't help feeling a little betrayed. Aunt Mof had known all along about the move, and she hadn't said a thing.

"My friends are here," I said, stomping the floor, like my friends were under my feet.

"I know it's hard," Mom said. She moved over to put her arm around me.

I stood and stepped quickly out of her reach, pacing and not daring to say all the angry words that flooded my mind.

"Scott and Carlos aren't friends that can just be replaced," I almost shouted.

"I understand that you're upset . . . but just try to calm down," Dad said in a tone that held a warning.

I paced a moment more and then sat again. "Dad, do you *want* to move to Cleveland?"

Dad hesitated long enough that I knew the answer before he spoke it. "We've lived here since you were born, Michael. No, I don't *want* to go, but I don't see any other way."

"Okay, what would it take for us to stay?" I started to pace again.

"We've explored every possibility. There just isn't enough business here."

"But what would it take?" I was pressing, but I felt desperate.

"Well . . . Michael," Dad said, heaving an exasperated sigh, "we've prayed about this decision for a long time. God would have to provide us with at least five significant contracts in the next month for us to stay, and . . . well . . . frankly, I don't see it happening."

"Five contracts in the next month," I said almost to myself.

"Five *significant* contracts," Dad corrected.

"Okay, big ones," I muttered, wondering if miracles still happened.

Dad stood and leaned over to examine my knees before he left the room.

"Come," Mom said, "have pizza. Yours is in the oven." She followed Dad out.

As soon as Mom cleared the doorway, I had my computer flipped on. I signed on the Internet and waited for the familiar connection sounds. Clicking on my e-mail option, I sent one short message and then signed off.

I swiveled the chair around again and sat for several minutes. There was a long silence before Aunt Mof said, "I wasn't sure until tonight." She adjusted her hair with her glasses and sat staring at the floor in front of her.

I just heaved a sigh. What could I say?

"Well," Aunt Mof started and then stopped.

I looked up, waiting.

"Well . . . your dad did leave a faint light of hope, I guess."

"Yeah, five big contracts," I said with a heavy heart. "It would take a miracle."

Aunt Mof brightened some. "Right, it would. But we believe in miracles, don't we?"

I wasn't so sure, but I nodded and shrugged.

"Tell you what," she said, with a little more enthusiasm, "give me a little time and maybe we can come up with something."

It seemed hopeless to me, but I nodded again.

"Go have your pizza and clean up . . . then come back here before you go to bed."

She waited with an expectant look until I nodded again.

Stacy joined me in the kitchen as I was putting pizza slices on a paper plate.

"We're getting a new house," she said brightly, obviously happy about the whole idea.

"No we're not!" I shouted.

She puckered up and poked her chin up in the air. "Mom says we are."

"You can go to Cleveland," I said slowly and deliberately, "but I'm staying here."

Stacy left the room looking upset, and I took my pizza and a cola and sat out on the back steps to wait. Right away Henrietta joined me in the growing darkness and offered the affection and sympathy that I needed right then.

"It isn't fair," I said, holding a slice of hot pizza in one hand and stroking Henrietta's head with the other. "No one considers my wants or needs," I complained. "No one cares that my whole life will change. No one cares that I'll hate Cleveland." Henrietta seemed to care, but it didn't make me feel any better. After several minutes I gave her the last slice of pizza and tossed the paper plate in the general direction of the garbage cans. I heaved many long sighs before I heard, a block away, the rumble of the faded blue Camaro.

"¿Qué tipo de e-mail *fue ese?"* Carlos asked, as he and Scott joined me on the dark steps.

I stared blankly at him until he repeated, "What kind of dumb e-mail message was that?"

"Just what it said," I answered. "We're moving to Cleveland."

"Cleveland?" Carlos repeated.

"Ohio," I said.

" I *know* where Cleveland is."

"No way, Prickett." Scott said, sounding as if he were unable to grasp the possibility.

"Well, that's what Dad says."

"But why?"

"Better job."

"Just for more money?"

"I guess."

"No," Scott said slowly, "we can't let it happen."

"Well, I don't know how we'll stop it." My voice started to quiver a little.

For several moments the only sounds were the crumpling of cellophane paper as Carlos unwrapped a mint. The three of us sat on the back steps for another fifteen minutes, speaking very few words.

"What about your aunt?" Carlos finally said. "Maybe she can talk to your dad."

"I doubt it, but she did ask me to come back to her room in a while."

"Vámanos," Carlos said, standing up. I didn't have the energy to argue.

As soon as we stepped into Aunt Mof's room, I was sorry we had. She had the history cards in her hands, and she wasn't one to be easily distracted.

"Sit, sit," she said, as though she had been expecting all three of us.

"Awwh, I'm just not up to it right now."

"We thought maybe you might have some ideas on how to keep Mike's dad from moving to Cleveland," Scott said.

"I'm working on it," Aunt Mof said, "but your history exam gets closer every day. I'll have a plan for you to consider by tomorrow. I promise. Okay?" She paused until we finally nodded, and then before we could get out of our chairs, she was drilling us on exam questions.

"What was the common name for the containment policy?"

"It was . . . uh . . ."

"Truman Doctrine. What city was blockaded by the Russians in 1949?"

" . . . blockaded? . . . uh . . ."

"Berlin. Name the Soviet-dominated military alliance formed in 1955."

We all shrugged.

"Warsaw Pact. What was the common name for the containment policy?"

"Truman something . . ." I said.

"Right. Truman Doctrine."

We heard that one again in a few minutes along with about fifty more. Aunt Mof was relentless in her effort to help. She finally let us go, and we gratefully escaped the grip of history.

Carlos looked at his watch. "The time . . . it's late. We go."

"We'll come up with something," Scott assured me weakly.

"Yeah," I answered, knowing it was unlikely that anything would change Dad's mind.

An hour later the house was quiet and dark except for the glow from the TV. I lay on my back holding my new trophy and staring at the ceiling, emotionally drained and wondering if teenagers could die from stress. I felt crushed by more than my share of it. I faced a history final that would determine whether or not I stayed on the tennis team; I was carrying around the guilt of a stolen exam; my girl wasn't speaking to me; and now Dad wanted to move me five states away from my best friends. I couldn't help wondering if God cared.

Saturday morning I woke up to cartoons. I didn't say a word as I glared at the girls from the sofa.

"Mom said we could."

I made a move to get up, but my knees had practically turned to stone overnight. I should have expected it. They were stiff and forming nasty scabs. I let out a howl and fell back, getting the girls' full attention. Stacy and Miranda hadn't seen the injury, and they were compassionate and sympathetic despite my nasty disposition.

"Want a bowl of Corn Pops?" Stacy offered.

I didn't. Miranda let Henrietta in, and she climbed up onto the sofa with me.

I lay back for a while, rubbing her ears and thinking of the chores I had to get done before I was free to take off with Carlos and Scott. The garbage had to go out, the grass had to be cut, and the tool shelf in the garage had to be cleaned up and organized. With a lot of effort I managed to get up and get dressed. I poured myself a bowl of Corn Pops and leaned against the kitchen cabinet to eat. Sitting was out of the question. I took the garbage out and carried the cans to the street for the Saturday pickup, and then straightened up the tool shelf. The lawnmower was super hard to start, and I moaned again over the fact that *everyone* else had a riding mower and I still had to use a walk-behind. I looked at my knees and debated asking Scott or Carlos to mow for me. Well, I wouldn't actually ask—I'd sort of groan and make it clear that it caused me a lot of pain to push the mower. And knowing that I couldn't leave the house until my work was done, Scott or Carlos—or both—would take over.

"Quit whining," I chided myself. I pushed the mower out of the garage and filled the tank with gasoline.

An hour later I finished the yard and was heading to the kitchen for a drink when I heard Carlos's car. He sat so low behind the steering wheel that only the top of his shaggy head showed. Perfect timing, I thought.

"What'd your aunt come up with?" Scott asked when he and Carlos found me in the kitchen.

"Haven't seen her."

"Well, let's go," Scott said as he turned to go through the living room and down the back hall. He looked ready for action, moving in a cowboy stride with his elbows bent.

Carlos and I followed him to my room. Aunt Mof was in her wheelchair typing on her laptop computer.

"Ahhh, boys," she sang out cheerfully, reaching over to pick up the stack of history cards. I couldn't believe it.

Awwwh . . . give it a rest, Martha, I thought; this is Saturday.

"Uhh, we just came to talk about the plan . . . uh . . . you know . . . the plan to keep Mike here," Scott said. He looked with disbelief at the cards in Aunt Mof's hands.

"I know you did, and I do have a plan. I've just been working on it," she said, gesturing toward her computer. "But, hey, we need to take every opportunity to prepare you for the history exam." Counting cards from the tall stack, she said, "When you know these fifty, I'll tell you about a plan that just might work."

Without giving anyone time to object, she started: "What pact was broken by Hitler on three occasions?"

"Munich Pact," Scott answered boldly, clearly pleased with himself.

"Right . . . good. What does *blitzkrieg* mean?"

"Blitzkrieg? . . . " Carlos thought out loud.

"Blitzkrieg means *lightning war*." Aunt Mof answered her own question.

"In what year did France fall?"

"1944?" Carlos guessed.

"No—1940. What was the title given to October 24, 1929?"

"Black Thursday," I said, trying not to act as pleased with myself as I felt.

"Right. What does *blitzkrieg* mean?"

"Lightning war," Scott answered, glowing.

Aunt Mof stopped suddenly, lifted her chin, squinted her eyes slightly, and sniffed before she stuck her hand out in Carlos's direction. After only a moment's pause, Carlos's face flashed a grin as he dug deep in his pocket and dropped a cellophane-wrapped mint in her hand.

We covered five sets of cards in the next half hour, going over each set of ten a second time once we knew them. The short stack was growing.

"Good job . . . okay." Aunt Mof took a deep breath, put aside the cards, and looked directly at me. "The problem, as you know, is that your dad hasn't been able to get enough contracts to keep the business at the level he feels necessary to pay expenses and provide for his family. You understand that."

I nodded.

"Your dad is very talented in reorganizing businesses, bringing dead companies to life—he's one of the best—he does good work and has a very good reputation." We all nodded, and she went on. "However, as competent as his work is, some potential customers just don't go out looking for his services—even those that really need help—and some prospects just aren't attracted by commercial advertising."

I couldn't tell where this was leading, but Aunt Mof sounded persuasive. We listened, waiting for the part where we'd get involved.

"Your dad has many strengths," she said. "But he isn't aggressive enough on a one-on-one level. Sometimes advertising doesn't reach the people who need to look you in the eye to understand how you can help them."

I still didn't know where this was leading, and the expressions on our faces must have said so.

"If you," she said, pointing to each of us, "want to help land five contracts,"—*five big contracts,* I thought—"then you'll have to help find the business people who need the one-on-one eye contact."

Aunt Mof leaned back and folded her arms in front of her like she was waiting for us to jump up and run out to find these people who needed the eye contact.

I was only beginning to have a vague idea of what she had in mind. Scott and Carlos shuffled their feet and shifted around in their chairs uncomfortably. I had the unpleasant feeling that if I didn't say something positive about the idea within a moment or two, Aunt Mof would whip out the history cards again.

"Sooooo? . . . okay," I said slowly, "how would we find these people?"

"You knock on doors. Just go out looking."

I was sure I couldn't do that, but I hesitated to say so.

"I couldn't do that," Carlos said.

"Sure you could," Aunt Mof said, looking at all three of us. "We'll make up fliers that give all the information you need, and all you'll have to do is hand them out to business people."

Well, that didn't sound too hard. If it meant staying in Cross Springs, I'd do it.

"But," I said, thinking more about it, "we don't know anything about small business consulting. How could we talk someone into putting a lot of money out on something we're so ignorant about?"

"You don't talk anyone into anything," Aunt Mof said. "All you do is hand out fliers and ask the business owner or manager to let you make an appointment for him or her with your dad. Your dad will do fine from there. It's the initial contacts that he could use some help with."

"Dad knows about this?"

"Uh . . . ," Aunt Mof said. "Not exactly."

I couldn't help smiling at that.

"He'll know eventually, of course . . . when you three start bringing him business. Now, the first thing you need to do is to make up a flier on the computer. I've been searching the Internet for information on small business reorganization."

She held out five or six printed pages.

"Especially emphasize this part," she said, holding up one of the pages. "It gives short testimonials about percentages of financial increase after using a business consultant. And here," she said, handing me the phone book, "look at all the information your dad lists in the phone book in his display ad."

The three of us leaned over the book. Dad had a big layout in the yellow pages.

"Okay," she said, "just take the information you have and arrange it in a readable form. And remember, your potential client wants his information concise and easy to read . . . no microscopic print or clutter all over the page."

I was sure Aunt Mof could do a much better job on this than the three of us could, but I reluctantly took the internet printouts, and the phone book, and flipped on my computer.

As we started reading over all the information we had piled in front of us, Aunt Mof slowly rolled her wheelchair out of the room and down the hall, saying, "I think I'll have lunch in the kitchen today."

Almost two hours later we found Aunt Mof in the family room reading to the girls. We sat and impatiently listened to the last half of *Little Red Riding Hood* before she sent the girls off and turned to us.

"All done?" she asked.

Scott handed her the flier, and we waited for words of praise.

She looked it over for quite a while, first nodding and humming, "uh hum . . . " and then pinching her eyebrows and her lips together. I couldn't tell if it was passable or not.

"Good job," she finally said, ". . . lot of effort here."

We relaxed some.

"But let's go back to the computer and make a couple of small changes."

Another hour of hard work left our flier looking entirely different than the original effort, but much easier to read. I was right; Aunt Mof would have done a better job the first time.

"Well?" she said, leaning back in her chair and looking at us with an expectant sort of expression, "Are you ready?"

Scott took a step back. "You mean now?"

I grimaced a little on the inside, not looking forward to the awkward embarrassment of having to talk to business people we didn't know.

"Why not now?" Aunt Mof asked, "You're prepared. Go do it. Take this flier to the convenience store and make about a hundred copies, and then just go from business to business asking for the owner or manager. Hand them a copy, mention a few details on the flier, and ask if you can make an appointment for them with your dad. Nothing to it."

It didn't sound like nothing to me, but we reluctantly shuffled down the hall. I wished we were on the tennis courts.

"Oh," Aunt Mof hollered after us, "your mom is at the mall. Please ask the girls to come back here with me."

Five minutes later I was easing my long legs carefully into the back seat of Carlos's car. It was a challenge to keep them stretched out.

"You gonna do business like that?" Scott said, pointing at my knees.

He was right. Only five-year-olds ran around with skinned up knees. I sat there several moments debating my options before I eased back out of the car and went to find a pair of jeans.

I came out the back door stiff-legged a few minutes later and climbed back in the car, gritting my teeth and breathing hard.

Our first stop was the convenience store, where we invested in twenty copies of the newly created flier. We weren't as optimistic as Aunt Mof. Scott and Carlos took care of making the copies while I sat perfectly still in the back seat.

My mind drifted back to that day—a lifetime ago—when I was ten, sitting alone in my treehouse. The overwhelming goal of my life at that moment was to be a teenager and have all the freedom I saw teenagers having—driving around aimlessly with friends, spending their own money, and coming and going as they pleased. Well, I'd made it, but it was no picnic. Involved in a theft that could get me kicked out of school—or worse—and within weeks of packing up and leaving my best friends forever. For a few moments I longed to be ten again.

"¿Adónde?" Carlos asked when he was back behind the wheel.

"Oh, pick a place," I said, feeling that one would be as useless as another.

Carlos took off and drove about a mile to the main part of town. Cross Springs was a fairly small place to be only an hour south of Atlanta. Azaleas bloomed everywhere in bright reds and shades of purple. Pink and white azaleas lined the sidewalks at the high school. It was a great place to live, and I sure didn't want to leave. It was funny how I'd notice flowers when I felt gloomy. Mom called it melancholy.

"Try here," Carlos said, pulling to a stop in front of Bagwell Plumbing.

"No way," I said, motioning for him to get going. "Kathy Bagwell's dad owns that place."

"So?" Scott asked.

"Kathy Bagwell's dad shot a guy once for bothering him."

"Awh, that was before we were born, and the guy was threatening him." Scott shook his head slowly.

"I don't care."

We drove around another fifteen minutes before Carlos stopped in front of Smyth-Carlson Hardware Store.

"I wouldn't talk to that guy for *two* significant contracts."

Scott and Carlos both twisted around in their seats to stare at me.

"Why?" they both asked at the same time.

"About two years ago Dad ordered paneling from Smyth-Carlson. It was delivered in colors that didn't exactly match. Mom hated it, and Dad ended up taking the guy to small claims court to get his money back."

We drove on.

"I know," Carlos announced. "Corey Johnson's mom runs a daycare center over behind the McDonald's on Third Street."

"Yeah," Scott said, "Corey says her mom never has enough kids."

We drove over to Third Street and found the place. *Closed on Saturday.* Scott got out of the car and shut the door.

"Closed, *ignorante*," Carlos shouted through the open window.

Scott ignored him and walked across the street to the McDonald's.

Over French fries and Big Macs we considered our options. Cross Springs had hundreds of small businesses, but none seemed to shout, "Come talk to me."

"Okay, look," Carlos said. "Next place, you just go in. No more excuses."

I wasn't convinced, but I didn't argue. It was already getting late in the afternoon.

The next place Carlos stopped turned out to be Ann's Beauty Shop.

"What'd you stop here for?" I tried not to whine.

"It's as good a place as any. Go." he said.

I hoped no one was watching from behind a hair dryer as I struggled out of the car.

"Go on," Scott urged, handing me a flier. I stood still, studying the flier for several moments, trying to think what I'd say. Finally I made my way to the door and knocked.

"Just come on in, honey," a large lady in huge pink curlers said, about the time I realized that I shouldn't have bothered knocking.

This is the dumbest place in the whole town to stop, I thought, looking over a row of hair dryers and ladies in weird hair contraptions. I was speechless, aware that every lady in the place was staring at me. Finally, I offered the flier to the lady who had told me to come in, hoping that she was the manager.

"Well, what is it?" she asked, glancing up from the paper in her hand. I tried to look her in the eye.

"Uh," I said, wondering if my new high school in Cleveland had a tennis team. "I'm Mike Prickett, and I'm passing out information for Prickett Small Business Consulting." She looked back down at the flier and nodded, so I went on. "I wonder if you'd be interested in hearing about how financially reorganizing could build up your business?"

She looked up, surprised. "Honey, if I had any more business, I'd have to put 'em in the closet." Then she laughed at her little joke, and several of the other ladies laughed with her as I realized what I should have seen right away. The place was packed.

"Well," I said with forced calmness and authority, "please keep this flier in case you need it in the future."

Then, in case they were watching, I walked slowly and deliberately back to the car, and then climbed quickly into the back seat trying to ignore my stiff knees.

"Let's get out of here," I said between clinched teeth.

I was repeating exactly what had happened in the beauty shop when Carlos pulled up to a barbershop about half a block down the street.

"What are you doing?" I was still stinging from the humiliation of the last stop.

"Look," Scott said. "No customers. None."

"I can't do it again," I mumbled, slouching down in the seat.

"You want to move to Ohio?"

He was right; there were no customers in the barbershop, so I reluctantly forced myself out of the back seat again. I took a deep breath and made my way slowly to the door—this time I didn't knock.

"Hi. I'm Mike Prickett," I said, holding out my hand.

A very bald barber quickly wiped his hand on his apron and then grasped mine in a firm handshake. I began to go through the same spiel I had bombed out on at the beauty shop.

"His name is Carl Braden," I told Scott and Carlos almost half an hour later, "and he's planning to retire and close the shop next month."

"Then what took you all day?" Carlos said. "It's hot out here."

"I think he gets bored in there without much to do," I answered. "He told me all about his daughter and her five kids in Florida. He's moving there when he retires. I just couldn't get away. I give up," I said. "Let's go home."

"One more stop," Carlos urged.

An hour and a half later, I was recounting to Aunt Mof what we had accomplished—or failed to accomplish. "After the barbershop we went six more places, and none of them—not one—wants a follow-up meeting with Dad."

"Hmmm." Aunt Mof sat thinking for a while, and we kept quiet.

"Exactly what did each one say?" she finally asked, picking up a pencil and a blank note card.

"Two already use a consultant," Scott said.

"And three do their own research and planning, and they're fine about that," Carlos said.

"That last place just said he couldn't afford it," I sighed.

Aunt Mof asked for the names of every place we went to and encouraged us to be patient and try again Monday, and then, just as we stood to leave, she did exactly what I expected her to do.

"Carlos," she called, "who was the founder of positivism?"

Carlos looked first at me and then at Scott before he heaved a big shrug and fell into the chair.

"Auguste Comte," Aunt Mof said, ignoring Carlos's exasperated expression.

"Who was the Prophet of the Social Gospel?"

"Rauschenbusch." Scott answered within his allotted three seconds.

"Walter Rauschenbusch. Yes, correct. Name the Canadian educator who was a contender for Fundamentalism."

"T. T. Shields," I quickly said.

"You got it!" Aunt Mof shouted like a game show host, and then went on immediately to the next question.

After close to an hour of drill, she let us go. It was dark out, too late for tennis.

"Necesito irme," Carlos said, and rather than walk home, Scott left too.

Chapter 7

Mom woke me from a sound sleep Sunday morning. "We need to leave here in less than an hour," she said.

"What?" I mumbled, sleepy and momentarily disoriented.

"Sunday school and church. Hurry and get moving."

I was too comfortable to move. "Aww . . . Mom, my knees are so stiff and miserable that I just can't wear long pants today. And I don't feel so good," I moaned.

She felt my brow and hummed a sympathetic little sound. As she walked back to the kitchen, I pulled the cover up around my chin and settled back for another hour or two of sleep.

"Your mom said to get up!" Dad threw me a towel.

I was up and in the shower in less time than it took to say, "Yes, sir!"

Two hours later, just after Sunday school, I slid into a pew beside about a dozen other teens. Mom and Dad and the girls found their usual places about halfway to the front. It took me all three verses of the first hymn to study my immediate surroundings.

Scott was sitting with his folks, and Carlos didn't usually come to our church, but I was sure he'd make it to the evening youth rally. This was a once-a-year well-advertised event.

". . . so make Eric Ranize welcome," I heard the pastor say as my attention shifted back to the pulpit. Then I remembered. Eric Ranize, the youth evangelist from somewhere up North. He spent several minutes plugging the evening meeting and encouraging everyone to bring their friends. I looked around, wondering if Amber had come. I expected her for the evening program for sure—after all, she had suggested that she'd see me at the get-together afterward. I mentally snapped to attention when I heard Pastor Ranize say, " . . . and so for the next six evenings—at seven P.M.—determine in your heart to make this youth rally a priority." What? Six evenings? Six? It was a week-long youth revival? Sorry, I won't be able to make it, I determined firmly as I mentally dug in my heels.

"It's never been a week long in the past," some guy sitting next to me leaned over and whispered, sounding as annoyed as I felt.

"I know," I mumbled. The evangelist sat down, and the senior pastor returned to the pulpit, making eye contact with me. I kept quiet the rest of the service, focusing first to one side of the pulpit and then the other.

I noticed her just after the final "amen," and I stood with my mouth open for a few seconds. She saw me too and made her way toward me, weaving through the crowd in the aisle.

"Michael," Mrs. Valbueno called out, sounding surprised and looking pleased to see me.

"Oh, hey . . . I mean . . . hello," I stammered. I might as well have been nailed to the floor. I was speechless.

Mom and Dad appeared behind her. "Mike," Dad said, "introduce us to your friend."

"Uh . . . Dad . . . Mom . . . uh . . . this is my history teacher, Mrs. Valbueno." Mom stepped in right away and introduced herself and Dad, and she gave Mrs. Valbueno a warm smile. I saw Scott about ten rows up; he wasn't making any effort to come any closer.

"What's she doing here?" Scott said in a hushed voice when I joined him in the foyer several minutes later.

"No idea," I mumbled.

A few minutes later, Dad and I sat impatiently waiting in Dad's black Mustang for Mom and the girls. When we finally saw them coming, Mom was walking with Mrs. Valbueno and pointing directions. I sank a little lower in the back seat when I heard Mom say, "Oh, just follow us. It isn't far."

Getting in the front seat, Mom said, "I hope you don't mind, David; I asked Harriet to dinner."

Harriet? I thought. Her name is Harriet? . . . and they're on a first-name basis already?

"No, of course not," Dad said. It wasn't unusual for Mom to invite dinner guests after church, and Dad never minded.

Miranda and Stacy shoved their Sunday school papers at me to admire, and they talked all the way home. I sat, thinking of Harriet. My history teacher coming to my house for Sunday dinner. I couldn't believe it. I knew why she was coming, and I deserved it.

"You're certainly quiet, Michael," Mrs. Valbueno said as I tied off the garbage sack half an hour later. Mom had called me from the family room where I'd been straining to hear the conversation in the kitchen.

I put a clean plastic liner in the container and stammered, "Yes, ma'am; I guess I've been busy . . . " I gave a nervous little laugh and wished I hadn't come into the kitchen. Aunt Mof sat in her wheelchair, peeling potatoes in a big bowl in her lap and taking up half the space in the kitchen. Mom was setting the table in the dining room, and Mrs. Valbueno was standing near the sink, making a salad. The three of them were chatting like old friends.

"How long has Mr. Valbueno been in the nursing home?" Aunt Mof asked.

"Almost six weeks now, and it's been a lonely and difficult experience for both of us. I'm there every morning . . . often making me late to class," Mrs. Valbueno said with a sad, faraway look.

"Well, we'll be praying for his fast recovery and return home," Mom said, putting her arm around Mrs. Valbueno's shoulder.

"The doctor says it'll be another month."

"Doctors are limited. I'm so glad that God isn't," Mom encouraged.

Mrs. Valbueno brightened some. "I should have started back to church years ago."

It sounded like a good time to make an exit. I carried out the garbage and then went around to sit on the front porch. At our house everyone uses the back door.

Henrietta followed and sat next to me on the steps. "She's going to talk to Mom and Dad about the stolen exam. I just know it," I whispered, rubbing the dog's long curly ears. "Maybe she's done it already." It was like torture, just waiting. Waiting and wondering when the bomb would explode.

Maybe I should bring up the subject first and get it over with. It could all be explained, but I was pretty sure that no one would sit through the whole explanation. It would be impossible to tell the entire story and make myself come out looking like an innocent victim. I did start out innocent, but then I'd deliberately gotten involved. I sure wished I hadn't.

I closed my eyes, braced my elbows above my scratched-up knees, and rested my chin in my hands. I sat there rocking slightly back and forth for several minutes, just thinking.

"What's she doing here?" Scott whispered, startling me out of my thoughts.

"What're you doing here?" I said in a low voice, matching Scott's.

"I saw her follow you. Why's she here?"

"You know why she's here," I said, feeling even more downhearted.

"Has she said anything yet?"

"No, but she will."

Scott made a fist and pounded it into his palm. "I was hoping maybe they'd just let it go."

"Yeah, right," I said with a snort. "Fat chance. You want to stay for dinner?"

"Very funny," Scott said, getting up to leave. "We'll pick you up at 6:30."

I sat on the front porch another ten minutes before I heard Dad calling.

"Put this on the table, please," Mom said, handing me a pitcher of iced tea as she turned to take the roast out of the oven.

Conversation at the table was lively and animated. Mrs. Valbueno was obviously enjoying herself, and everyone seemed especially talkative.

"Michael," Mrs. Valbueno said, drawing me into the conversation, "I'd love to see your new trophy."

"Mikey has hundreds of them," Stacy said.

"Michael has twelve," Dad said, with obvious pride.

"Well, I'd love to see them all."

"Pass the butter, please," I said, looking toward Aunt Mof, and trying to change the subject.

After dessert, I helped clear the table and then escaped to the family room. I put on the earphones and turned on the CD player.

I'd listened to the music for some time before I sensed that I wasn't alone in the room. I instantly bounded off the sofa, almost ripping the earphones off. I expected the confrontation—my heart was pounding.

"Oh, I'm sorry," Mrs. Valbueno said quickly, putting her hand on my shoulder. She sounded sincere. "I didn't mean to startle you."

"No . . . uh . . . no . . . I just didn't . . . uh . . . no problem," I stammered.

She picked up the trophy from Friday's tournament. "Beautiful, absolutely beautiful," she said, slowly turning the little statue over and over in her hands. "And what about this one?"

she asked, looking at another one. I gave a very brief account of every trophy on the mantle, hoping to hurry the conversation.

"Your family is so kind, Michael," she said, handing me Friday's trophy and turning to go. "You must be very proud."

I couldn't tell if she meant proud of the trophies or proud of the family.

"You have to leave already?" I heard Mom say a few minutes later.

"Hank will be expecting me."

Mom handed Mrs. Valbueno a small wrapped plate holding two slices of apple pie.

After hugging Mom and Aunt Mof, Mrs. Valbueno left before 3:00. As far as I could tell, she hadn't said a word about the exam.

Feeling restless, I went to the computer to check my e-mail. The sign-on process took only a minute or two. "You have mail," the computer's automated voice chimed. Actually, I had a lot of mail. I hadn't checked it in two days. Most of it was advertisements that I deleted without reading. But there, almost at the bottom was one from AMBERDELL.

The last time I'd seen Amber, she turned away and didn't speak, so I was a little uneasy about what she might say now. Clicking on her name, I read, "Hey Mike, Congratulations on the tournament. I'm looking forward to the youth rally tonight. I'll save you a seat." She signed it, Amber.

I sat at the computer for a long while, not sure how to answer, or what to think. Just like Mrs. Valbueno, Amber seemed to have forgotten the problem of the exam. It was a problem that I was sure would surface again. But when? And how? It seemed that anytime I had an opportunity to talk to Dad, I had avoided it. It was like walking a razor-sharp line. On the one side I hoped that Scott and Carlos were right and the problem would just be forgotten, but on the other, I doubted that was possible. I'd deal with it later.

So, Amber was inviting me to sit with her. Maybe I'd enjoy the meeting after all. I suddenly felt a lot better about having to go.

Just after 6:30 I heard Carlos's rattletrap rounding the corner.

"See ya', Mom," I yelled as the screen door slammed shut.

Carlos and Scott were eager for a detailed report as soon as I got in the car.

"Not a word about anything," I said.

"Well, what do ya' figure she has in mind?" Carlos thought out loud.

"I don't know. I can't think about it anymore," I said, closing the subject.

We drove slowly past the tennis courts. Two were vacant. Carlos motioned toward them. "Sure you wouldn't rather be there?"

I turned to watch the singles match and wondered what Amber would think if I didn't show up.

We parked on the street near the church. We were twenty minutes early and already the parking lot was full. Two busses from other churches took up about six or seven parking spaces. I had expected a crowd, but this was a surprise.

"Hi, guys." Stephanie fell in step with us as we headed for the back entrance of the building. "How are your knees?" she whispered.

"A lot better," I said. "Which church do you go to?"

Stephanie stopped suddenly. "I've been visiting here for two weeks, Mike," she said with a big smile. "It's you who haven't been around lately."

Only Stephanie's smile and friendly tone of voice kept me from cringing with embarrassment.

Taking advantage of the opportunity, I filled in the silence, "Well, if I'd known you were here, I'm sure I'd have been here." The moment I said it, I was sorry. I knew what was coming.

"Well, I'll save you a seat," she said with a smile, and turned to join her girlfriends.

I stared straight ahead, my mind racing. Amber and Stephanie were both going to save me a seat. Now what was I supposed to do? I shuffled along with Carlos and Scott, engrossed in my latest problem and beginning to develop a headache.

"Come on," Scott said, as I slowed down, trying to delay the decision. "The back row will be full if we don't get on in there."

Maybe the whole place will fill up and the girls won't be able to save me a seat, I thought, hopefully.

"Save me a place," I said, as I ducked into the men's room to think. I leaned against the cold tile for a long time, knowing that both Amber and Stephanie were wondering where I was. How could I have let this happen, I wondered. Maybe I was making too much of it. Probably there was a perfectly reasonable and obvious solution. If there was, I wasn't smart enough to see it. Carlos and Scott didn't know about Amber's invitation, and I didn't think they had heard Stephanie, so they didn't have a clue about my absence either.

I left the men's room when I heard the music and the first chorus. I paced the foyer for a moment or two and then stood looking through the crack between the swinging doors. I spotted the girls on either side of the center aisle, and each one had left a seat vacant next to her. I was considering walking home when I heard Mr. Richwine say to someone, "Kyle isn't here. He's supposed to usher tonight."

In a flash I saw the answer to my problem. "I'll usher," I said, stepping quickly over to Mr. Richwine.

"Oh good, Mike. Thanks."

I got my instructions and then joined Scott and Carlos to wait for my signal to join the other student ushers in handing out visitor cards, and later, to take up the offering.

After three or four more lively choruses, Mr. Richwine walked to the pulpit, ready for his usual job of making announcements.

Dennis Richwine was a large man, about Dad's age, who seemed to be the brains behind just about every coordinated activity the church held. He knew where things were and who was to be doing what. I was holding down the dangling end of Carlos's shoelace with the toe of my shoe so his lace would untie the next time he moved his foot, when I heard my name from the pulpit. Jerking to attention, I listened to Mr. Richwine say, "Mike Prickett will be taking Kyle Dekker's place with the ushers this week."

No, no, I silently protested, *not all week—just for tonight.* Carlos and Scott both turned and looked at me with raised eyebrows and questioning looks. I stared straight ahead, pretending not to notice them. Well, at least Amber and Stephanie would understand my absence. Later, I'd straighten out Mr. Richwine about the rest of the week.

"Welcome visitors," Mr. Richwine boomed in a loud and sincere voice.

That was my cue to stand and join the ushers at the swinging doors. We each picked up visitor cards and slowly started down the aisles as Mr. Richwine asked the huge auditorium of mostly visiting teens to make themselves conspicuous by raising their hands.

I wouldn't have done it. And neither did about half the visitors in the auditorium.

As I came even with Amber's row, I caught her eye and gave a very slight, helpless shrug. She flashed an understanding smile and a moment's eye contact that said, *Oh, Mike, I understand. We'll get together another time—probably many times*. Well, that's what I imagined she was thinking.

Turning to look for visiting hands in the section across the aisle, I saw Stephanie several rows ahead, and prepared to share the same meaningful exchange with her.

Stephanie also seemed to understand why I wasn't sitting next to her, and her expression was also a promise of future times together.

Within ten minutes the ushers were trooping down the aisles again—this time with collection plates—and again I exchanged meaningful glances with both my girls.

"Laura died just three weeks ago." Eric Ranize had our total attention. He had been introduced and had stepped up to the pulpit. Now he left a very long silence while every teen in the auditorium began to feel uncomfortable.

"But Laura was prepared to die," he said slowly, in an expressive voice of total relief.

I think we all felt relief, but dead was dead.

"Laura was seventeen." Another pause. "And Laura was my niece."

Pastor Eric—he said to call him Pastor Eric—went on to tell how Laura was driving her dad's car and in an instant her life had ended. If his strategy was to create an emotional rain forest—it was working. Looking around I saw several of the girls fishing around in their purses for tissues. Guys don't tear up, but sometimes tears don't show.

I picked out two or three guys whose expressions gave them away, but sitting near the back row, I could only see a few faces across the aisles.

I wondered about Cleveland, and then my mind was on my girls. My girls, yes, I could see Amber about ten rows ahead. Uh . . . no . . . twelve rows ahead and five seats over. My view of Stephanie was blocked by some big football player type.

Pages were flipping and Pastor Eric read, "And as it is appointed unto men once to die, but after this the judgment . . . Hebrews 9:27."

I looked over at Scott's Bible and then found Hebrews about the time Pastor Eric called out II Peter 2:9. He paused and then started reading, "The Lord knoweth how to deliver the godly out of temptations, and to reserve the unjust unto the day of judgment to be punished."

I was familiar with the verses Pastor Eric was reading. I'd been in church all my life, but somehow I wasn't in any frame of mind to seriously consider them. Amber had mentioned the gathering at Michelle's house twice. Michelle's parents often had the teens in the church over Sunday evenings, but Carlos and Scott and I didn't usually go. This time, though, I was looking forward to an hour or so with Amber.

I felt Scott's elbow jab my ribs, and my attention snapped back to my Bible.

If we confess our sins, he is faithful and just to forgive us our sins, and to cleanse us from all unrighteousness.

Well, I thought, stealing an exam sure qualifies as sin. And trying to cover it up isn't much better. I knew that problem wouldn't just fade away, but I hoped to delay its settlement for a while longer. I had quit thinking about the probable consequences.

Over and over I dragged my attention back to what Pastor Eric was saying, and over and over I'd drift off again.

Some guy right in front of me had a hole in the back seam of his sleeve. It was about an inch long and between a red and blue stripe. He was half again my size, and I figured that one good flex of those muscles could spread that little rip another two inches.

Suddenly, everyone was standing and I quickly joined them, glancing around to make sure we were *all* standing, not just a group answering an altar call. I'd sat through many altar calls—I'd even answered a few—but tonight my mind was on other things.

The service lasted another half hour and then there was an altar call that seemed to touch dozens of teens. For all I'd gotten out of the service though, I could have stayed home. But then, if I'd stayed home, I'd have missed my date with Amber. Well, of course it wasn't really a date, but maybe it would lead to one.

We filed out into the aisles and cleared the auditorium in minutes. Small groups headed for fast-food restaurants and big groups drifted toward the two busses. The regulars from our church gathered in the foyer, and it occurred to me then that Stephanie might be planning to go to Michelle's house too. My suspicion was immediately confirmed when Stephanie and Michelle walked in together, laughing and chattering like best friends.

"Well, Mike," Michelle said, "we haven't seen much of you lately. I'm so glad you're here." My chest tightened, and I forced a plastic smile, desperately trying to sort out my options.

"Coming to the house tonight?"

I didn't have time to duck into the men's room to think this time.

"I'd like to," I said apologetically, "but I've got a ton of homework." As I said it, I glanced around, making eye contact with six or seven people, including both Stephanie and Amber. I deliberately avoided looking at Scott and Carlos. We had been planning to go together to Michelle's. I couldn't tell if the girls admired my studious attention to academic priorities, or if they thought I was a dumb bozo for waiting till Sunday night to study.

I made a quick exit, followed by both Scott and Carlos.

"¿Qué tienes?" Carlos asked.

I couldn't tell him and risk being laughed at.

"Oh, nothing." I shrugged. "I just don't feel like going."

"Well you did two hours ago," Scott insisted.

"And disappearing for fifteen minutes and then showing up with an usher's badge?" Carlos said.

I kept walking across the dark parking lot in the direction of home. "Y'all go on," I said with a jerk of my head, ignoring the questions.

They went back to the group, and I walked the two miles home alone, thinking and feeling sorry for myself. The cool night air held the faint smell of smoke—burning memories of dead winter twigs and limbs, long overdue for the flames. The last faint flickers of daylight were gone, and the long street ahead was dark and moonless—silent, except for the distant howling of some unhappy dog.

Homes were faintly outlined shadows with an occasional dim light from a window. Garbage cans sat at the curbs ready for early morning pick up. The creaking of a porch swing and the faint outline of a white shirt left me straining to see Mr. Hammond. My footsteps on the sidewalk were quiet.

Crossing Adams Street, I could see the interstate several blocks away, car headlights leading the way home after a long day in the city. Muted laughter drifted from the back yard of the Levandoski home, and soft humming seemed to come from somewhere—probably old Mrs. Wilson.

These people are my neighbors, I thought—this is my home. I couldn't imagine starting all over.

As I walked up our driveway, I could see that the house was dark except for the light in my bedroom. Aunt Mof was, of course, home. I assumed that Mom and Dad and the girls were still at church.

I used the hidden key at the back door, grabbed a cola, and headed back to my computer.

"Oh, you're home earlier than I expected," Aunt Mof said, clicking the mute button with the TV remote. The room smelled of chocolate, and an open box of assorted candies sat on the bed.

"Yeah," I said with a shrug.

"Ummm . . ." she hummed, "and you don't look too happy about it."

I just shrugged again and heaved a sigh as I sat down in front of my computer.

After I sat several moments without turning the computer on, Aunt Mof said quietly, "Want to unload?"

I needed to unload—a lot of frustration was piling up, and I was having trouble sorting it all out. It was a risk, but I took a chance on Aunt Mof.

It took me a while to get started, but I told her about the evening and about Amber and Stephanie and how I had become the new usher for the week.

Aunt Mof listened without interrupting, nodding now and then, and when I finished she sat quietly for a long time.

Finally she said softly, "Michael, I wish I knew how to advise you."

I couldn't help feeling surprised at her response. She took my frustration seriously, yet she wasn't leaping in telling me how to solve the problem or telling me how dumb I was to get into the mess in the first place.

"Well, maybe one of the girls won't come tomorrow night," I said.

"I'll be praying that God will work it out for you His way," Aunt Mof said.

I heard banging at the door and let Scott and Carlos in. We walked to the back of the house.

"You didn't stay long," I said.

"Nah, got boring," Carlos said, and waved hello to Aunt Mof as she reached for the history cards. I wasn't surprised. I'd been expecting her to drill with the cards again.

"Hah, just what I expected," Scott said good-naturedly.

We spent about forty-five minutes on fast-paced, animated questions and answers before Aunt Mof laid the cards in her lap for a moment and said, "You guys are doing great. If we keep this up, there's no doubt you'll ace that history exam."

"If we're even allowed to take the history exam," I said quietly and deliberately, keeping my eyes focused on the floor.

I glanced at Scott and Carlos, and both of them were studying the carpet too.

"Ummm . . ." Aunt Mof said, "would this have anything to do with an original copy and initials in blue ink?"

I quit breathing for a second and glanced over at the guys. They were pale. It was confession time, and Aunt Mof was waiting.

"Well . . ." I paused to give the guys time to object. They didn't say a word, so I continued. I began with the envelope Scott had taken to the copy room, told about taking the exam and then trying to return it, and then ended with the reaction of the students and teachers. Carlos and Scott both interrupted over and over to add to the story. I didn't come out looking like any innocent victim.

When we finished, I felt exhausted, and none of us spoke, waiting for Aunt Mof to express her disappointment and tell us what to do and when to do it.

But she was quiet for a while, then she said, "Where is the exam now?"

"Torn in little pieces and flushed in the gym bathroom," I answered, barely above a whisper.

"Well," she said, "you're right; you do have a major problem."

She waited for us to nod our agreement, which we did.

"And you obviously regret the whole thing."

Again we nodded eagerly.

Aunt Mof put her finger against her lips for several moments, thinking. She glanced at me. "When I was a girl, I remember your grandma saying hundreds of times to your mom and me, 'Two wrongs don't make a right.' "

Now where had I heard that before.

"Have you confessed to God and asked His forgiveness?"

I shifted in my chair, beginning to feel uncomfortable again.

Reaching for her Bible, Aunt Mof said, "Let me share just one verse with you."

Then she read I John 1:9. "If we confess our sins, he is faithful and just to forgive us our sins, and to cleanse us from all unrighteousness."

It had a very familiar sound. Pastor Eric had read the same verse a couple of hours ago.

"No lecture, guys." She smiled with a sad and sympathetic expression. "But you know what you ought to do . . . okay?"

We nodded, moving toward the door, eager to escape.

Later, after Mom had put the girls to bed and Dad had finished with his newspaper, I sank into the sofa in the family room.

Minutes later both of them were standing near me.

"How was the meeting?" Dad wanted to know.

"Big turnout?" Mom asked.

"It was okay, and the place was packed," I said, yawning. "I'm really tired."

They took the hint and left as I reached up and flipped off the lamp, turned on my CD player, and adjusted the earphones. I was tired all right, but much too wired up to sleep.

Henrietta settled on the rug beside my bed and nuzzled my shoulder, begging for attention. "Hey," I murmured, "no one put you out?" I reached down and stroked her head and back for a long time, thinking of all that had happened since the fiasco with the exam copy.

"Aunt Mof is right," I whispered to Henrietta. "The sooner we get the mess out in the open, the sooner it'll be over with." Besides, if we're going to get kicked out of school, I'd just as soon go before we spend another zillion hours learning history cards. I was sure Henrietta agreed.

I lay thinking about Cleveland and wondering how my life would change there. We had one possible way of escaping the move, and that was the plan Aunt Mof had worked out. We hadn't done any good on our first trip out, but maybe my method or my introduction had been wrong. For several minutes I tried to work out a new way of introducing myself.

Laura was only seventeen, but she was prepared to die. The thought was an unwelcome interruption. I didn't want to think about Pastor Eric's niece, or death, or sin. I was tired. I wanted to make plans for tomorrow. Okay, let's see . . . , I'll call on more businesses and hopefully find at least one who will talk to Dad. Maybe I should phone first and make appointments.

. . . It is appointed unto men once to die, but after this the judgment. The words burned in my mind, uninvited. I sat up, and Henrietta jumped up on the space I'd just cleared.

I'm a born-again believer in Jesus Christ, God's Son, I told myself. So why do I feel like I'm not? Abruptly, I got up and went to Mom and Dad's bedroom door. I paced the hallway for several minutes and then padded back to the sofa. Wait, I thought. Just wait for the right time.

I couldn't sleep, and every time I tried to think, Pastor Eric's evening message echoed in my mind. I pushed Henrietta back onto the floor, turned on the CD player, and flopped down on the sofa again.

The Lord knoweth how to deliver the godly out of temptations, and to reserve the unjust unto the day of judgment to be punished.

Maybe Cleveland is my punishment, I thought suddenly. Nah, probably not. Henrietta scratched at the door to be let out. "So I'm keeping you awake," I muttered as I opened the kitchen door.

Half an hour later I was still sitting up, clutching my pillow and bracing against the fragments of thoughts that kept flying at me.

Chapter 8

When the obnoxious ringing of the alarm clock forced me to my feet only a few hours later, I felt drugged. Sometime in the early morning hours I had finally given up and given in. I wasn't sure what I had given in to, but after deciding to do the right thing about the test, whatever that was, I had relaxed enough to sleep.

Twenty minutes later Mom called from the kitchen, "Breakfast in five minutes."

I zipped my backpack. "Okay," I mumbled, looking at my bed. Even after a shower and my weekly shave, I knew I'd fall asleep in thirty seconds—if I could just get back on that sofa.

Aunt Mof was at the table putting butter on toast when I came in. She looked at me several long seconds. "Were you up all night?" she asked.

"Almost all night," I said, reaching for the box of Corn Pops.

Mom came over and took a closer look, then felt my forehead. "Hmmm," she murmured, "no fever."

Mom diagnoses just about every kind of sickness with her hand to the forehead.

"I'm fine," I said. Actually, I wasn't fine at all. I figured that I'd be talking to Mr. Fielder today, and I wasn't looking forward to it.

Half an hour later, I joined Scott and Carlos, and the three of us ambled toward the high school.

I thought of Pastor Eric and the youth meeting and wondered if Carlos and Scott had come to the same conclusion I had.

"Probably we'd better get it over with today," I said, looking at the sidewalk and deliberately stepping over the cracks.

"Maybe," Scott said slowly. He sounded like he really meant "probably not today."

"Look," Carlos said, his accent more noticeable than usual, "Mrs. Valbueno forgets—so we forget, *¿no?*"

"Yeah," Scott added. "Let's just sit on it. Not lie, of course. Just wait."

I didn't answer.

Carlos kicked a pine cone out to the middle of the street and said firmly, "Don't fan the fire. The tournament was last Friday. If they're going to bring up the issue of the exam again, it'll be today. See. So, if we get through today, we got it made, *¿no?*"

"Right," Scott said. He shot his fist into his open palm and looked as frustrated as I felt.

After a long pause, I mumbled, "I guess." I'd be perfectly happy to never think about the theft again, ever. But I knew I'd keep thinking about it until it was settled. Waiting until everyone forgot about it wasn't settling the problem.

The bell rang just as we found our places in Mrs. Valbueno's room, and two minutes later she hurried in.

"Good morning," she said, and most of the class responded.

She called the roll, not giving any clue in her voice that she remembered singling us out last week. Strange. Like it was all over and forgotten.

"Final exam is a week from Thursday. I hope you're working on the review questions." Mrs. Valbueno looked around the room. The three of us nodded enthusiastically, thanks to Aunt Mof.

"Class review starts next Monday. Oh, and I've made up a new exam from the four hundred and nine review questions," she said.

I held my breath for a moment, looking straight ahead, but Mrs. Valbueno didn't seem to have us in mind, and she kept going. "We'll see a video today." She went on to tell about the biography we were about to see. I relaxed some, eager for the end of the semester and the three-week break between semesters.

An hour later, out at our lockers, Scott held Carlos's books while Carlos struggled with his lock again.

"Get a new lock, DeSantos."

"*Ves, hombre,*" Carlos said, "not a word about the exam."

"And she's making up a new test, so even if we *had* studied it, there wouldn't be a problem," Scott added.

That sounded like pretty stupid reasoning, but I didn't say so. I didn't say anything.

"Hey," Scott said quietly, in a tone of voice that caught my attention. I glanced at him and followed the jerk of his thumb. Amber was rounding the corner, heading our way.

"See ya' later," I said, dismissing them both. I began to organize my locker again.

Amber joined me, silently standing there, smiling.

"Hey," I said, searching for the right words.

She reached over and pulled my English book from my locker. I couldn't help feeling pleased that she knew I had English next period. Amber had English, too, but hers was an honors class down the hall from mine.

"We missed you last night," she said in a soft, friendly tone. She smelled like roses, and I breathed deeply.

Ah, the get-together at Michelle's house, I thought.

"Thanks," I said, and thought frantically for a way to change the subject.

"Been working on the 409?" I asked, hoping she'd been impressed that I'd skipped a party to study.

"Some. I guess you'll be at church tonight. You being an usher an' all."

"I guess." I hesitated, knowing it would be hard to get out of it now that Mom and Dad considered me committed to the job.

"Well, actually . . ." she said. I waited expectantly without a clue about what she was thinking. "Stephanie and I both missed you."

I think I quit breathing.

She laughed and held up the palm of her hand in a "stop" pose. "It's okay," she said, still laughing. "Really."

I didn't know whether to laugh too or to beg forgiveness. As I searched for the right words, she went on. "Stephanie is coming with her boyfriend tonight."

"Oh," I said, feeling stupid. It never occurred to me that Stephanie might have a boyfriend.

"So . . ." She paused. "Well, can I save you a seat—for after you do the ushering stuff?"

"Sure!" I began to breathe again. "Sure, yeah, thanks." I couldn't help the big dumb grin on my face as I closed my locker and glanced at my watch.

We hurried down the hall, and I paused as Amber turned toward the door of her classroom.

"Oh," she said, and handed me my English book. She held the book about two seconds longer than she had to, and somehow those extra seconds made my heart pound. I could hardly wait for the youth rally.

After fourth period, we headed for our favorite bench in the courtyard. Scott slowed his steps, mumbled something I couldn't understand, and pointed slightly with his chin.

I looked toward the double doors. "Here he comes," I whispered, my mouth going dry.

"Hello, boys," Mr. Fielder said a moment later. It was hard to judge his mood or tone.

"Hello, Mr. Fielder," we said together, and for a moment I felt like Stacy and Miranda the day they got caught with a handful of the neighbor's prized roses.

"We need to talk."

"Yes, sir?" Scott answered and asked at the same time.

"Sit down."

We sat, and I swallowed five or six times in the next ten seconds. Pretty hard to do with a dry mouth. I was sure I had guilt written all over my face. Scott looked cool and unconcerned.

"Boys," Mr. Fielder said, then he paused for a long time as if he were thinking. "I need to ask you again about the history exam that was taken from the copy room."

Carlos had predicted that today would be the day. Where was he? I slid my eyes toward the cafeteria, and then instantly back to Scott.

"Yes, sir," Scott was answering, sounding sincere and concerned about Mr. Fielder's problem. "We've all heard about the stolen test. You haven't found it yet?"

Scott was handling Mr. Fielder like an artist squeezes a piece of soft clay. Mostly it was his confident and concerned tone of voice. I watched, both amazed and appalled at what I was hearing.

Scott went on. "There's a lot of talk around campus about that exam. Hard to imagine anyone at this school doing such a stupid thing." Then, just as skillfully, Scott turned to me and with a slight motion of his hand, indicated that it was my turn to confirm our innocence. Mr. Fielder took the cue and also looked at me.

I said as casually as I could, "Yeah, Scott even saw the test in the copy room that Tuesday." It was amazing that I could even speak, with my mouth feeling like cotton, and my chest caving in from lack of oxygen.

Carlos arrived and handed Scott and me our sodas. "Hello, Mr. Fielder."

"Carlos." Mr. Fielder acknowledged, as he just nodded.

He nodded several more times as he stared at a candy wrapper in the grass—probably considering how far to push—and then abruptly he said, "Have a nice day, boys." He turned and walked back toward the double doors.

"Oh boy, oooh boy, oooooh boy," Scott murmured, frozen in place as his eyes did funny things. "That was close."

"*¡Sí!* . . . *pero* . . . it's over," Carlos said in a very low voice, popping the top on his can. "They no bring up again."

I looked from Carlos to Scott and back to Carlos, relieved that it was over. But the issue wasn't really settled. I found myself wondering if Scott and Carlos were really Christians. And I didn't let myself think about my own standing before God.

I'd come to school prepared to tell the truth and take the consequences. Now, I was probably in for another all nighter.

At the three o'clock bell, we left P.E. class and the tennis courts and headed to Carlos's house to pick up his car.

"Stop by the convenience store," Scott said. "Let's get more copies of this flier."

As much as I hoped this plan worked, I didn't look forward to calling on more businesses. It sure hadn't done us any good on the first trip out.

"We'll go back to the daycare first. You go in there and come out with a promise of a call to your dad," Carlos said, in a really bossy tone.

You go get slapped around at a few businesses and see how eager you are to go back, I thought. But . . . any way you looked at it, this was our best hope. Our only hope.

We got a hundred copies of the flier and headed for Johnson's Daycare over on Third Street.

"We wait," Carlos said, as he pulled into the McDonald's parking lot.

I looked across the street to the daycare center and reluctantly started off, rolling up the flier loosely and rehearsing my introduction. The wind whispered through the needles of the tall Georgia pines that covered the front yard. I couldn't see through or over any part of the fence, but it sounded like a hundred little kids were back there playing and screaming.

I stood at the door, putting off the inevitable as long as I could. I remembered my humiliation at the beauty shop on Saturday, then I walked right in. I stood in a very small foyer, only about six feet square. Two padded folding chairs and a little table with magazines filled the small room. A half door was straight ahead, the bottom half closed so the preschoolers couldn't escape. Looking past it, I could see through sliding glass doors out to the back yard where about a dozen little kids were playing on swings, throwing balls, and running around.

"Well, hello, Mike." Mrs. Johnson suddenly appeared from a small room to the right—her office, I guessed. "You need to see me?"

I was surprised that she remembered my name. "Yes, ma'am," I said with all the confidence I could fake. I unrolled the flier and offered it in her direction.

Mrs. Johnson looked at the flier for a few seconds without taking it, then motioned toward her office and quietly said, "I'm in a client meeting right now. I won't be long; can you wait?"

I didn't want to wait, but I nodded and sat down, looking around the closet-sized room and listening to the yard full of screaming, laughing preschoolers. I crossed and uncrossed my legs, stood up and looked out the sliding glass doors a few moments, and then sat again as I looked at my watch. Five minutes. How long did she expect me to wait?

About the time I was thinking of leaving, the office door opened a little and a very small person peeked out. A sandy-haired girl about three years old, I guessed. Her blue eyes were large and were the exact color of her oversized T-shirt. For several moments she just looked at me—staring until I began to feel really uncomfortable. I picked up a magazine and pretended to read, lifting the pages until they blocked my view of her.

I heard the door click shut, and I relaxed a bit until I realized that she had stepped out and was standing near me. Imagine being intimidated by a three-year-old.

Immediately the door opened again—several inches—and a voice said, "Stay where I can see you, Angela." The door remained partly open.

I was ready to bolt.

"What's your name?" the bold one asked, never taking her eyes off me.

"Mike."

"Mike?"

"Yeah."

For several more long moments she stood looking me over.

"I have new shoes," she finally announced.

"Good," I said, pretending to study the magazine.

Angela inched over to the chair next to mine and climbed up. Then, getting up on her knees, she hovered over me for a better view of the pictures. I offered her the magazine, and she took it and sat down as I got up to pace.

Come on, come on, I silently grumbled as I looked at my watch. Ten minutes. I gotta go.

"Okay, Angela," Mrs. Johnson said, smiling as she came out of her office. "Would you like to play in our yard with the other children tomorrow?"

Angela moved next to her mother and wrapped both arms around her mom's legs.

"We'll be here in the morning," Angela's mom said as they left the building.

"Well, Mike," Mrs. Johnson said, looking at the flier again. "What have you got here?"

I spent the next few minutes going over the highlights of the flier and giving a glowing report on Prickett Small Business Consulting.

"Hmmm . . ." she hummed as she read again all the points I had just explained. "I may call one of these days, Mike, but a consultant is so expensive. I have a license for twenty-five children, and I have only twelve, no, thirteen right now. Probably when I get more children I'll be able to afford it better. But . . . I'll keep this." She gave the flier a little shake and put it in a drawer.

"Twenty minutes for nothing." I slid into the booth next to Scott and wolfed down the last handful of his French fries.

"Vamanos," Carlos said, standing and searching his pocket for his keys.

"I'm thirsty," I grumbled.

"Later," Scott said as we left the building.

"Look," Carlos announced when we were in the car, "maybe this works, maybe not, but let's don't do it halfway. Give it all you've got or forget it." He sounded as frustrated as I felt.

In the next half hour we called on nine or ten businesses. I heard the same old excuses. "I'm going to reorganize by myself, or I use such-and-such consulting company, or it's too expensive." We wrote down all the businesses and their responses as Aunt Mof had instructed.

At 4:30, we were still batting zero when Carlos let me off in front of Eddie's TV and VCR Repair. I took a deep breath and prepared for another rejection as I stepped in the door.

When my eyes adjusted to the light—or lack of it—I looked around a store about twice the size of Mrs. Valbueno's classroom. I could hardly believe the junk and clutter. Hundreds of TVs and VCRs lined the floor and filled the aisles. They were stacked on top of each other and piled up on tables and shelves. The place smelled dusty and looked dirty.

Before I saw anyone, I heard the grunting, straining sounds of someone struggling and frustrated. I spotted a huge black man across the room just as he muttered something under his breath. He, (Eddie, I later learned) was sitting in a wheelchair balancing a large TV in his lap and trying to maneuver the wheel of his chair around a small VCR that was partially blocking the aisle.

I was embarrassed to be seen staring at the wheelchair, and Eddie looked angry and embarrassed at being stared at.

"Whadaya want?" he asked in a furious booming voice that filled the whole room.

I stared at the wheel stuck on the VCR, and the muscles in my arms flexed as I mentally lifted the TV from his lap. I stood still, unable to speak for a moment. My natural instinct was to instantly help with the TV or the wheel, but I doubted that he wanted help.

"Whadaya want?" he repeated.

I wanted to leave, but I kept staring at the wheel as I fumbled for the right words.

"I'm looking for an after-school job," I said, flabbergasted at the words I heard myself speaking. I just couldn't imagine this big angry man calling Dad to discuss reorganizing his business finances.

"A job," Eddie said with a snort. "Not a chance."

For some reason I had an almost uncontrollable desire to help the man in the wheelchair.

Why was I still in this place? I looked around in disbelief and walked closer to the wheelchair. "I work cheap."

"I've hired kids before. You don't want to work; you want to play."

"No, sir. I work." I reached over and lifted the TV from his lap.

I stood holding the TV for several seconds as I looked around for a place to put it. Every flat surface in the entire store was occupied by some broken or torn-apart TV or VCR. Eddie freed his wheel and then reached up and took the TV from me.

"I've got friends in the car out there," I said. I jerked my thumb toward the front of the store. "Give us an hour, and we'll have the aisles clear, and this place organized." I wondered what Scott and Carlos would say to that idea.

Eddie looked skeptical and then pointed to a wide ledge on the wall about as high as my head. "See that shelf up there. Clear it off, dump all that junk in the dumpster out back, and put this TV up there."

I folded the flier, stuffed it in my back pocket, and had the shelf cleared and the junk in the dumpster in less than five minutes. I had to struggle and huff some to get the TV heaved up above my head and on the shelf, but I didn't let the struggle show.

"Well?" I said when the job was done.

Eddie looked pathetic and angry at the same time. He stared at me for a long time—probably trying to decide if I was jerking him around, or really needing a job.

"Get your friends," he finally said. He moved the wheelchair and bumped into something else that blocked the aisle. "Start with that far wall and carry everything on those two shelves to the dumpster."

Rather than explain the whole situation and spend ten minutes coaxing the guys to cooperate, I just opened the door, caught their attention as they sat listening to the radio, and motioned for them to come on in.

I was standing next to Eddie when Scott and Carlos walked in.

"Carlos. Scott," I said, looking first to one and then the other as an introduction.

"Eddie," the big man said. It was the first time I heard his name.

"Guys, we're going to spend an hour and make this place shine," I said, as I made my way over and around pieces and parts of TVs and VCRs. "We'll start with this wall and clear it." I handed Carlos a small TV, then stacked two old VCRs in Scott's arms and sent them to the dumpster. I went out with my own load as they came back for more. I was careful not to be outside at the same time they were. I'd explain later.

We had the entire wall of old and outdated equipment in and around the dumpster in less than twenty minutes. Then, under Eddie's supervision, we began clearing the main aisle in the store—putting repaired TVs on the high shelf and ready-to-be-repaired TVs and VCRs on the working level shelf. From time to time Eddie would point to another pile of junk for the dumpster.

"What about this stuff?" Scott asked, holding up a box of tools and old instruction manuals.

"The storage room is around back, left of the dumpster," Eddie said.

Scott struggled with the box and was doing some pretty heavy breathing when he left the building.

Eddie had Carlos sweeping the newly cleared aisle when Scott reappeared at the back door several minutes later with a tall ladder and two long fluorescent tubes.

The change in the place was dramatic with the addition of the two tubes. After an hour, the wheelchair could move freely in the aisle—only the main aisle—and with the far wall organized the place was looking more like a business that really meant business.

"We gotta go," I said, thinking of the youth rally and the seat next to Amber.

Eddie got out his wallet and peeled out three ten-dollar bills—it looked like all the money he had—and began to talk. "I've been in business here seventeen years," he said. "For the first five years, mine was the only place in town to take your TVs for repair. I had five employees and more business than we could handle. I'm good." He stopped and looked at the three of us standing quietly, shifting from one foot to the other. "And then there was an attempted robbery that left me in this chair."

Eddie took a long, slow breath, and I figured he must have been remembering the events leading to the wheelchair.

I couldn't have explained my overwhelming desire to help this man. It was more than pity—it was more like my own need to help. I didn't intend to do it, but I found myself pulling the folded-up flier from my pocket and offering it to Eddie.

He unfolded it and studied it for several moments. I looked around and admired the improvements we'd made.

"So that's it," he said. "You didn't want no job."

From Eddie's tone, I realized I shouldn't have given him that flier. But, still trying to help, I knew that Dad could improve Eddie's business.

"I can guarantee you more business if you'll call my Dad," I said, hoping Dad could pull it off.

"Not a chance," Eddie said flatly. He folded the flier and handed it back to me.

"How about if we hand out fliers for your business tomorrow and bring you five new customers?" I asked, as Carlos and Scott backed toward the door.

Eddie looked up and smiled broadly. "Five customers?" he said.

Several minutes later, I joined Scott and Carlos out on the sidewalk.

"¿Estás loco?" Carlos exclaimed.

"You're out of your mind," Scott said. He raked both hands roughly through his hair.

"I know, I know," I said. They were right. I must have been nuts. But I still intended to try to help Eddie.

"Look. It won't take long. We'll make up some brochures on the computer—sort of like this," I said, holding up the folded flier. "We'll just pass them out here in front of his store for an hour or two tomorrow after school."

"WE?" Scott shouted, again. "Don't say *we*."

"Okay, I'll do it myself," I said, walking away in a huff.

I walked a block and a half before Carlos pulled up to the curb near me. It was too far to walk home, so I got in the car and allowed myself to be lectured all the way to the house.

Chapter 9

I scanned the auditorium as I slid into the back pew. Amber wasn't there. I kept looking, jerking my attention back to the double doors several times when latecomers slipped in.

"Welcome," Mr. Richwine was saying to the crowd after the first song, and I took my cue and joined Nathan, Nick, and Caleb at the swinging doors to pass out visitor cards. Every night there would be fewer first timers, but we'd catch three or four.

Back in my seat a few minutes later, I stared at the floor in front of me. *She's not here*, I kept thinking. She said she'd save me a seat, and she isn't here. I did see Stephanie sitting next to Marshall. He wore a smile two sizes too big. Annoying.

Carlos jabbed me in the ribs, and I quickly picked up a song book and flipped to the right page.

A few songs later we took up the offering, and I couldn't help scanning every row again, just in case I'd missed her. But I knew she wasn't there.

"Turn with me to Romans 12:2," Pastor Eric was saying, and my attention drifted toward the pulpit—for the moment.

And be not conformed to this world: but be ye transformed by the renewing of your mind, that ye may prove what is that good, and acceptable, and perfect, will of God.

Pastor Eric paused several moments as his eyes skimmed the audience. "God's perfect will for your life will make you happier, more fulfilled, and more content than any plan you could ever dream of on your own," he said in a booming voice that snatched back my wandering attention.

Well, I sure don't want to go to Africa or somewhere like that, I thought, remembering missionaries telling about God's call on their lives.

Maybe she didn't have a ride. I wished I'd offered to pick her up. I could have borrowed Dad's car.

Pastor Eric went on and on about God's plan for our lives and how sin kept us from finding that plan. He read from Romans 7:15, *"For that which I do I allow not: for what I would, that do I not; but what I hate, that do I."*

Well that's me all right, I thought. I hadn't wanted to get involved with the stolen exam. But, I had. I hadn't wanted to deliberately mislead Mr. Fielder and Mrs. Valbueno. But, I had.

After another poke from Carlos, I flipped over to Philippians 4:11. Pastor Eric read, *". . . For I have learned, in whatsoever state I am, therewith to be content."*

Whatever state? I suddenly thought, and I focused intently on Pastor Eric for several minutes. Content wherever I find myself? Like maybe in Ohio? Was God putting this thought in my mind? I struggled to pay attention.

At 8:30, the three of us popped open soda cans and headed for my room to tell Aunt Mof about Eddie and the other business failures.

"Good meeting, boys?" Mom asked.

We only nodded as we sank into chairs.

"Hey, Mike," Dad called. He sounded really glad to see me.

Dad smiled at Scott and Carlos, but he zeroed in on me. "I got a call from Andy's Steak & Grill today," Dad said. I must have looked as blank as the door, so he went on. "Mr. Williams says you were by his place Saturday? Handing out some kind of brochure?"

"Oh," I said, feeling a growing excitement. "Oh. Oh, yeah. But he was one of those who said he couldn't afford a consultant."

"One of those?" Dad said, waiting for an explanation.

"Well, uh . . . David," Aunt Mof said. "You see, Mike and Carlos and Scott made up a flier and just showed it to a few business people in the area. Businesses that could use your help," she said casually.

I couldn't help looking at Aunt Mof and blurting out, "But he said he couldn't afford . . ."

"Well, I called him and convinced him to let your dad show him how it would be to his advantage to make some changes in his financial structure," she said with a shrug, like it was nothing at all. "So, David," Aunt Mof said to Dad, "did you get the contract?"

"We sure did." Dad beamed.

Carlos and Scott and I gave each other fierce pats on the back and confirmed our success by punching the air with our fists. "One down, four to go," Scott said with confident enthusiasm.

"What?" Dad's eyebrows drew together, and he looked confused.

Aunt Mof spoke up. "You said five contracts, and you could stay in Cross Springs."

"Oh. Oh yes. Well, I think I said five *significant* contracts. And it would take three of the Williams contracts to make a significant one," Dad said, sending a lot of our excitement right down the drain.

"Never mind," Aunt Mof said. "You'll get more." She said it to us, but she was looking at Dad.

"Dad," I said, "do you ever do any free work . . . you know . . . give your time and—"

"Pro bono?" he asked. "Sure, once or twice a year. Why?"

"Well, we met this guy, and . . ." I went on to tell Dad about the hour we spent at Eddie's place. "So, would you consider giving Eddie some free advice? You should meet him, Dad."

"Well, Mike," he said, "maybe under different circumstances, but right now I'm trying to tighten things up at the office and leave Frank with as few problems as possible when we leave. It would take hours just to study his books to give any advice at all."

"But . . ."

"Okay . . . *If* we leave," Dad said when he saw me clinch up.

"Now, don't get all riled up," Dad said slowly, preparing me—in his own way—for something I didn't want to hear, "but your mom and I plan to fly to Cleveland tomorrow. We'll spend one night and be back Wednesday."

"But, why?" I turned sharply to Mom and waited for an answer.

Mom didn't look any happier about the announcement than I did.

"Well, Dear," she said. There was that word again. I recognized the direction this speech would take. "Your dad has to make a quick trip to Cleveland." Mom paused and looked at Dad before going on. "And, well, he wants me to ride around with a realtor to look at homes in the area."

"We'll leave after breakfast tomorrow," Dad said. "The twins will stay with Shelia."

Dad left the room, and that was that as far as he was concerned.

The five of us were silent for several moments before Aunt Mof said to Mom, "Alisa, sit down. Maybe you should know what we're up to."

Mom sat, and Aunt Mof started explaining our plan. Scott and Carlos and I added details and then told them both about Eddie and the promise I had made him that afternoon.

"Do you really think it's possible to get the five contracts your dad needs?" Mom looked at me with a hopeful expression.

"Definitely possible," Aunt Mof answered for me.

"Then . . ." Mom paused, "maybe I could help."

"Sure," Aunt Mof immediately said. "Sure you can. In fact, I have an idea that we'll talk about later." Mom seemed to brighten a lot.

"I've got to pack," Mom said as she left the room.

"Did you list the places you stopped and note their reasons for not wanting to call your dad?" Aunt Mof got right down to business.

We gave her the scrap of paper, and she looked over it quickly and laid it aside. I saw the stack of history cards on the table next to her wheelchair, and I just wasn't in the mood, but she didn't reach for the cards.

"So, what about the TV place?" Aunt Mof asked, ready for more details on Eddie.

"Mike promised to hand out fliers for the guy tomorrow," Carlos said with obvious exasperation.

"And the purpose of that?" Aunt Mof asked, looking at me with her big smile.

I thought it was obvious, but I said, "To bring attention to his business."

"Right! So what could you do to draw attention to yourself so that the fliers would get into as many hands as possible?"

I felt that blank look coming on again. I didn't know what she was fishing at.

"Never mind. We'll get you the attention you need."

Aunt Mof reached over for the stack of history review cards, and the three of us sank reluctantly into chairs.

"Carlos," Aunt Mof said brightly, "name the top official in the state department who was indicted by Whittaker Chambers."

"Alger Hiss," Carlos shot back. The brightness of his eyes revealed the pleasure his slight scowl tried to conceal.

"Good! What Wisconsin senator was known for his investigation of Communist subversion?"

The three of us stared at our shoes.

"Joseph McCarthy. Who developed the hydrogen bomb?"

Aunt Mof talked fast when she did the history review, and often she'd get really enthusiastic. A correct answer within the allowed three seconds would almost bring her out of her chair. I could imagine her dancing around the room if it weren't for the casts on her legs.

The "short stack" of cards was now much taller than the original stack, and we felt pretty good about ourselves.

"I gotta go," Scott finally said after almost forty-five minutes of drill.

"Okay, guys," Aunt Mof said, "if you'll come here right after school tomorrow, I'll help you with the attention you need for Eddie's fliers."

"Tomorrow is early dismissal—teacher's work day—because exam week is coming up," Carlos reminded us. "We'll be here at 1 P.M."

By 10 P.M., Henrietta and I were sharing the sofa again. I sat with the remote and flipped from channel to channel. Eventually I lowered the volume on the TV, got out the CD player, and adjusted my earphones. It had been a long day.

"She wasn't there tonight," I said quietly to Henrietta, and then felt her lay her head on my chest.

I could feel the sympathy, and I needed it.

"She said she'd save me a seat, but she wasn't there," I said again, staring at the ceiling.

Pastor Eric's message earlier in the evening had been about avoiding sin and finding God's plan for our lives. It was hard to concentrate on God's plan for my life, with grades, and girls, and

Cleveland already weighing down my mind. Pastor Eric's voice floated through my head, *Not that I speak in respect of want: for I have learned, in whatsoever state I am, therewith to be content.*

I didn't think I could be content in Cleveland, but I figured God knew that. I must have made a strange sound, because Henrietta suddenly moved, wiggled out from under my hand, and headed for the back door.

Miranda woke me up early Tuesday morning. "We're going to Aunt Shelia's house today," she said cheerfully.

"Have fun." I turned over and immediately dozed off again.

"Bye, Mikey." Stacy tried to give me a hug.

It was still early—no way was I getting up for another half hour.

Several minutes later the girls were in Dad's car with enough luggage to keep them traveling for a week. Mom leaned over the sofa with her overnight bag on the floor and her purse hanging off her shoulder. "Keep your heart and mind pure before God," she said for the thousandth time as she cupped my face in her hands. "I left the keys to the Cherokee on the kitchen counter . . . just in case of an emergency."

I couldn't imagine an emergency big enough to get me in that pink thing, but I nodded.

After the family left, I poured a bowl of Corn Pops and took it to the family room and sat down to watch the cartoons that the girls had left on. I guess I got engrossed. When I glanced at the clock almost an hour later, I jumped up, grabbed my backpack, and ran down the street.

"You're late," Scott said, announcing the obvious.

We were very late to first period, but Mrs. Valbueno was even later. She came in two or three minutes after we had spread out our books and stashed the backpacks. Amber was there, her long brown hair pulled back with a big puffy yellow tie. I took out a sheet of paper and carefully drew out a large question mark, and then waited until I could catch her attention. It didn't take long.

She saw it, and I watched her tear off a piece of paper and start writing. She folded the note several times and then passed it across two rows to me. Holding the note made me remember the book she had held a second too long yesterday. I unfolded the scrap of paper and read, "My great-grandmother was rushed to the hospital in Atlanta. We had to go there. Don't you check your e-mail anymore?"

My e-mail. No, I hadn't checked my e-mail in a couple of days. But it wouldn't happen again. I glanced over at Amber and found her watching me.

"Mike!" Mrs. Valbueno said.

I jerked to attention, glad that I'd been called down and not Amber.

By 1:15, we were taking pizza out of the oven and heading to the back room.

"Thanks," Aunt Mof said. She took a big slice of pizza from the paper plate.

"So," Carlos asked, "what's the big attention getter?"

"It's good, real good." Aunt Mof smiled with an expression that was hard to read. "But first," she said, (and I knew what was coming) "let's spend about ten minutes on the cards." Between bites of pizza, she called out over two hundred history questions. We were getting faster and faster on the answers, and there were fewer of them every day that she had to repeat.

Half an hour later she put the cards aside and reached down to pull a long box out from under the bed.

"This," she announced, with a tone of triumph, "will get you all the attention you need."

With that, she opened the box and lifted out Mom's old clown costume. She held it up for us to admire, and for a few seconds we were properly impressed. She was right, that would get attention for sure. I remembered seeing Mom wear the costume at the twins' birthday party a couple of years ago.

It still hadn't dawned on me what she had in mind, but as she held it up, looking me in the eye, her mouth kind of pinching together as she tried to suppress a grin, I began to catch on.

"Ohhhhh NO!" I said slowly, holding my hands in a palms out, stop gesture. "Not in a million years," I said, beginning to back up a little. I felt beads of sweat pop out on my forehead. Aunt Mof was a very persuasive taskmaster, and chances were that eventually I'd be wearing that costume. Scott and Carlos knew it too and started to laugh and whack me on the back, calling me Bozo and other clown names.

"You do want to help Eddie draw attention to his business, don't you?" she said.

"I'd probably faint." I began to plead. "And I'd be the laughingstock of the whole school."

"Oh really," she said with no particular emotion.

"I just couldn't. I can't. I won't."

Fifteen minutes later, I sat in a chair facing Aunt Mof while she painted my face with clown white. She painted red circles on my cheeks, exaggerated high black eyebrows, and a big red mouth and red plastic ball nose. My huge puffy sleeves were two different colors, one red, the other yellow. The right side of my outfit was red and white stripes, and the left side was yellow with green dots. It was huge. Must have had a hundred yards of material in it—almost. Aunt Mof topped it all off with a fuzzy orange wig.

Scott and Carlos were enjoying nearly hysterical laughter until Aunt Mof suggested that she could find two more costumes.

I looked at myself in the mirror. "I feel like an idiot," I said to Aunt Mof, and there was just enough agony in my voice to bring a sympathetic response.

"You'll do fine," she said. "You might even like it. Besides, Eddie's waiting for you."

"You talked to him?"

"I got information about his store to make up this flier," she said, reaching for a piece of paper on the table next to her wheelchair. I'd forgotten all about making a flier. "You'll need to make a couple hundred copies on the way there."

Five minutes later I climbed into the back seat of the Camaro, hoping none of the neighbors were watching. "Let's get out of here." My nose itched, and there wasn't a thing I could do about it. "Let's go!" I yelled.

"No puedo," Carlos said, exasperated. "Won't start."

"What?" I shrieked. "What's wrong with it this time?"

"*No sé*. It's just dead. Probably the battery."

He and Scott got out and looked under the hood for a few minutes before giving up. Little beads of sweat formed under the thick layer of clown white. Carlos's car wasn't air conditioned even when it *was* running.

"Can we take your mom's car?" Scott asked.

"NO!"

"Aren't those the keys to the Cherokee in the kitchen?" he said.

"NO."

"It's too far to walk," Carlos said. "I'm getting those keys."

He got the keys and the three of us pushed Carlos's car out into the street so we could get Mom's pink eyesore out of the garage. I never dreamed it would come to this. I must have been out of my mind.

"You'd probably better drive it yourself," Carlos said. He tossed me the keys.

After today, I might be glad to move out-of-state, I thought. I got in the Cherokee and pulled my yards of clothes in with me.

I parked across the street from the convenience store and sunk down behind the wheel while Carlos and Scott went in to make copies of the flier. I couldn't tell if it was me, or the pink Cherokee, but both kids and adults took quick second looks and broke out in great big grins as they passed by. I should have parked behind the store.

It took them almost fifteen minutes in the store.

"You coulda made a thousand copies in all that time." I spun the tires as I left the curb, sending gravel and dust flying through the air.

I parked behind Eddie's place, next to the dumpster, and reluctantly got out of the driver's seat. I was scared, but as I stood there, I was also strangely excited. I followed Carlos and Scott through the back door of the repair shop.

"Well, I wondered when you . . ."

Eddie stopped cold when he saw me, then his entire face smiled. "Well, I've never seen such a . . . " he said. "I can't believe what I'm . . . " he tried again. "Is that Mike?" Eddie asked Scott, as though clowns don't hear and answer.

"¡Es cierto!" Carlos answered. "Here, take these out there and stir up some business." He handed me a stack of fliers.

I gave Eddie a flier and waited for his response while he studied it for several moments.

"Ummmm . . ." He nodded, obviously pleased, then looked at me and that smile filled his face again.

"Go on," Scott said, and I walked toward the front of the store, my stomach in knots.

First I looked out the grimy window as far down the sidewalk as I could see in both directions. The place was deserted.

Then I took a deep breath, opened the door, and stepped out on the sidewalk. For at least a full minute I stood waiting for someone to notice me. My chest pounded, and my breathing was uneven, coming in little jerky gasps. I knew Eddie and Scott and Carlos were watching out the window.

Suddenly, a door opened about twenty feet down the sidewalk, and a very tall, white-haired, elderly man came out carrying a small package and studying the sales slip in his hand. He glanced my way, then looked back at his sales slip for half a second before his head jerked back my direction again. Then, his face broke into a huge smile just like Eddie's. It was an automatic response. As I walked over and handed him a flier, my nervous feet were almost floating above the sidewalk. The old man walked on, glancing at the flier and turning every little bit to get another look at me. He hadn't said a word.

Within thirty seconds, a mother and three little kids pulled up in front of the bakery across the street. "LOOK," one of the kids screamed. "A CLOWN!" They waved and shouted and stared. I waved as I crossed the street and gave the mom one of Eddie's fliers. I wished I'd thought to bring a pocketful of candy. I offered my white gloved hands and shook with all the kids.

Like pigeons on a deserted beach, people began to appear from nowhere. The empty sidewalks became more and more busy, and I couldn't help wondering where everyone was coming from. Doors opened on both sides of the street, and salesclerks, storeowners, and customers drifted over for a closer look. I passed out Eddie's fliers and talked to little kids. I began to walk with confidence, going from person to person as if I knew exactly what I was doing.

It was clear that no one saw Mike Prickett, the klutz. They saw a clown. Only a clown, with all the built-in fascination and charm that's part of being a clown. I began to skip down the sidewalk. I hadn't skipped since I was five. I didn't know I could still do it.

There was never what you'd call a real crowd of people, but for almost three hours I made my way up and down the street in front of Eddie's place. I gave out his fliers and directed people to his store.

Sometime before the last flier was gone, I noticed someone taking pictures, but I paid little attention to the guy. It seemed natural to take pictures of clowns.

Twenty minutes later we were home. We all talked at once, shared details of the afternoon with Aunt Mof, and congratulated ourselves on a great job.

"Oh man, oh man, oh man," Scott said, shaking his head and running the fingers of both hands through his hair, "you shoulda seen that Mike."

"Yeah," Carlos said, "he was struttin' up and down the street like he owned the place."

"Well I'm proud of you, Mike," Aunt Mof said with real admiration. "I've been busy too, while you guys were out. I talked to Edith Wilson, your dad's secretary. She's going to help us set up appointments. So . . . you'll hand out the fliers and introduce Prickett Small Business Consulting, then your mom and I will follow-up on the promising ones, and Edith will make the appointments."

It sounded like a perfect setup to me. Dad would be totally surprised—but I expected him to be pleased.

"In fact," Aunt Mof said, with the expression of a grand prize winner, "I called Johnson's Daycare today. Mrs. Johnson now has an appointment with your dad Friday morning."

"But she said—"

"I know what she said," Aunt Mof answered, waving her hands in a "just-forget-that" motion. "I simply convinced her that with your dad's help she could fill those twelve vacancies much faster than she could do it alone. She's looking forward to the meeting."

We were impressed.

"Have you looked in the mirror lately?" Aunt Mof asked, starting to laugh.

I hadn't—but when I did I couldn't clean up fast enough. Sweaty clown white had mixed with red circles and black outlines to run in little trickles down my neck. Once we were on the way home, I felt free to scratch the itchy places. My face was a smear of red and black and white. I peeled out of the yards and yards of stripes and dots, then I looked around for a washcloth to clean up my face. Easier said than done. After twenty minutes of hard scrubbing with soap and hot water, I still had traces of white in my eyebrows and the hair above my ears.

After a short session with the history cards, we spent the next half-hour working on Carlos's car. We finally all chipped in and bought a new battery. It took another trip out in the eyesore to buy the battery. For months I'd avoided riding in that Cherokee, and now I'd driven it twice in one day.

Scott and Carlos left to get ready for the evening youth program, and I headed back to check my e-mail.

I found Amber's note about her great-grandmother. Her message was the same as she'd written in class this morning, except for the last line. "Let's try again Tuesday night."

Well, here it is Tuesday night, I thought. Just save me that seat.

An hour later, Scott found me in the family room in front of the TV with a plate of chips and a couple of hot dogs. "Can you drive tonight?" he asked.

"Drive what?" I asked, not believing he really meant for me to take the pink Cherokee again.

"Carlos's grandmother sent him on an errand; he won't be able to go tonight."

"Then we'll walk," I said, annoyed at the thought of Scott's suggestion.

"Okay by me." Scott shrugged and looked at his watch. "But we'll be so late someone else will have to usher . . . and you won't sit with you-know-who."

I parked the Cherokee a block from the church, and we hurried in just as Mr. Richwine started looking around for someone to take my place.

"Sorry I'm late—again," I said.

I looked for Amber through the crack between the double doors while Mr. Richwine struggled to get the usher's badge on my collar.

"She's in there," he said with an adult-sized grin.

I instantly turned away from the door, red-faced. Mr. Richwine gave me a friendly whack on the back and walked toward the front of the auditorium.

I spotted Amber about ten or twelve rows ahead when I joined Scott a moment later. As promised, she had saved a seat for me. I reached up and smoothed the back of my hair, brushed imaginary lint off my pants, and sat a little straighter. I kept thinking, *Let's get the offering over with.*

At the signal, I met the other guys at the double doors, and we walked the aisles with cards for first timers. Keeping a serious expression, I managed to exchange a glance with Amber before I returned to my seat for fifteen minutes of hymns and choruses.

Caleb handed me an offering plate when I found my place with the ushers after the music, and we walked the aisles again.

Amber looked up and smiled without embarrassment as I stood waiting for the plate to come back down her pew. Then I held her eye as she lifted up the plate.

Two minutes later I slid casually in beside her, my heart doing strange exercises.

"Hi," she whispered.

"Thanks for saving me a place," I whispered back.

Pastor Eric started talking, and I listened for the scripture reference, wanting to make a good impression.

I noticed the same rose-scented perfume that she wore every day at school, and I took a long, slow, deep breath. The puffy thing that held her hair back was pink this time and matched her shoes. I sat tall and struggled to pay attention to Pastor Eric. I wondered if maybe I should have used some of Dad's cologne or something.

"Turn to Psalm 37:39 and 40," Pastor Eric said, and I found the passage before Amber got her Bible turned right-side up.

But the salvation of the righteous is of the Lord: he is their strength in the time of trouble.

Pastor Eric began talking about ways that God helps us in times of trouble, when suddenly I realized that Amber was standing up. No one else—just Amber. I felt confused and disoriented for a second before I noticed Mr. Richwine standing in the aisle whispering to her and looking toward the back of the church where her dad stood. Something was wrong. I moved to join them in the aisle, but Mr. Richwine stopped me with a quick frown and slight shake of his head. I sank back down.

Five minutes. We sat together five minutes, and now she's gone and I'm stuck here alone next to people I hardly know. It didn't seem fair.

I didn't bother looking up any more verses. I suspected that Amber's great-grandmother was the problem, and I couldn't help feeling sulky.

Half an hour later I slipped out during the closing chorus and brought Scott out of the back pew with a slight jerk of my head. On the way out the door, Mr. Richwine caught up with me. "Mike," he said quietly, "Mr. Dellaney's grandmother died tonight, and the family had to go to Atlanta."

Chapter 10

Ignoring the racket at the back door, I sunk a little deeper into the sofa cushions and pulled the sheet up over my head.

"Do you know what time it is?" Carlos yelled, as he and Scott interrupted my unfinished sleep.

I glanced over at the clock, and flew off the sofa, grabbing my clothes on the way to the bathroom.

Thirty minutes later the three of us slipped quietly into Mrs. Valbueno's classroom, absorbing stares and a few snickers. Mrs. Valbueno made a note in her roll book, then went on with her lecture as though being twenty minutes late to class was an everyday event.

Amber was absent, and I missed her. Several times I glanced over at her empty desk and imagined her sitting there with the pink thing holding her hair back. Even though we missed the first twenty minutes of class, history seemed especially long today, and the stares and snickers continued.

"Michael," Mrs. Valbueno called when we stood at the sound of the bell.

As most of the class filed out to the hallway, we moved to the front of the room, ready to explain how my folks were out of town, and I'd forgotten to set my alarm.

"I'm impressed. Your parents must be very proud of you," she said.

I stood there with a blank expression as Carlos and Scott glanced at each other.

"The newspaper," she said.

We shrugged and shifted around.

"Oh my!" Mrs. Valbueno said, laying the palm of her hand against her face.

She went to her briefcase and took out the *Cross Springs News* and opened it on her desk.

I stared at the paper several moments before I could absorb and believe what I was seeing.

"You made the front page," Scott said, stating the painfully obvious.

There, in color (the newspaper seldom printed anything in color), was a huge picture of a clown in bright stripes and dots, handing out fliers in front of Eddie's TV and VCR. Faintly in the background, I made out the faces of Eddie, Scott, and Carlos through the dirty window. It wasn't exactly *The Atlanta Constitution*, but our small local paper would be in the hands of most everyone we knew.

Well, that explained the stares and snickers. I could expect them for the rest of the day.

"There's a wonderful write-up under the picture," Mrs. Valbueno said, beginning to read. "Michael Prickett, age 16, hands out advertising brochures for Eddie's TV and VCR. Michael, son of Alisa and David Prickett, of Prickett Small Business Consulting, works to help build up the family business."

Dad won't feel proud at all, I thought. He'll be as embarrassed as I am. Suddenly I was glad Amber was absent, and I hoped she'd be out a couple more days until the papers were gone and forgotten.

For the rest of the day, in classes, in the hallways, and at lunch, I endured exaggerated smiles and smirks—and a few choice clown names. "Hey, Bozo."

At 3 P.M., after a hard hour on the tennis courts, we walked to Carlos's house.

"We need a couple hundred more fliers," Scott said, picking up the last three or four from the back seat of Carlos's car.

"Couple hundred?" I gasped. "We'll get twenty." I was handing them out one at a time with at least a five-minute speech at each place.

"Okay, you're the one moving to Cleveland," he said with a shrug, and then waited for me to change my mind.

"We'll get thirty, then," I said, giving in a little.

For the next hour Carlos pulled up at business after business where he and Scott waited in the car while I went in and asked for the owner or manager.

"Ohhhh," I heard at least ten times, "you're the kid in the paper." And although it seemed to get me the extra attention I needed, I still heard most of the same reasons that they couldn't, or wouldn't, call Dad.

Back in the car, we wrote down every store name and the response I got inside. Aunt Mof would call some of them.

Next, Carlos stopped in front of Agar Pest Control. "Miguel," he said with the tone of a college professor, "maybe you need to change your approach."

"Yeah," Scott said from the back seat, "you need to go in with more confidence and enthusiasm. Like they should feel lucky to get a minute of your time."

"You wanna do this yourself?" I said, jerking my head around to see his face.

Carlos quickly focused his attention on something outside his window while I forced myself out of the car and walked, weighed down with the sudden criticism, toward the pest control office.

I took several deep breaths and stood a long time at the door before I opened it wide and stepped boldly in, wearing an especially big smile. I talked loudly and more animated than my natural voice when I asked for the office manager.

Startled by the interruption, the lady at the front desk, the only desk, paused before she said, “Yes, may I help you?”

This was always the awkward part. “I’m Mike Prickett, with Prickett Small Business Consulting,” I said enthusiastically, handing her the rolled up flier. Before I could go on, she, like the others, lit up with recognition. “Oh, you’re the . . .” She stopped and smiled. “I mean, I saw your picture.”

I started my rehearsed lines. “I’d like to—”

“Wait,” she said, waving both palms at me. “You need to talk to Mr. Agar.”

I glanced around. She was the only person in the room, and I didn’t see any other rooms.

“Mr. Agar owns the company,” she explained. “He’s here every other Wednesday, but he came and left early today. Sorry.”

So much for another one, I thought, annoyed at Scott and Carlos for making me put on this act.

The lady went on. “Mr. Agar’s main office is in Atlanta. He has small offices like this one in twenty-one small towns in Georgia.”

I was ready to leave when she picked up the phone. “I’ll call him for you.”

I hated to tell her to “forget it,” but I wished she would.

“Mr. Agar’s office please,” she said. “Cynthia, here—Cross Springs.” Cynthia looked up and smiled real big, probably remembering the clown picture.

“Mr. Agar? . . . yes, it’s Cynthia, at the Cross Springs office? . . . yes.”

She glanced at me and then sort of turned her swivel chair around a little so that it was hard to hear her muffled voice.

“Yes, sir. Prickett. The boy in the paper. Right.”

Cynthia went on to explain what I wanted, and then, as she spoke, she fed the flier into the fax machine. Before she finished talking, Mr. Agar had a copy of my flier in his hand.

"He can see you at 4:30 tomorrow," she said, and then waited for me to confirm the appointment.

"Uh . . . here?" I stammered. She had said he wouldn't be here for two weeks.

"Atlanta office," she whispered, holding her hand over the receiver.

"Well . . ." I paused, wanting to say "NO WAY," but not wanting to seem ungrateful for her efforts.

"Mr. Agar is very active in the Junior Chamber of Commerce," she whispered, encouraging me to say yes. "He supports kids in business."

"Okay, sure. Thanks," I said, wondering how I'd get to Atlanta.

I left the office with the Atlanta address and an encouraging lecture from Cynthia.

"Mikey's home," Miranda yelled, leaving her bike in the middle of the driveway, as I climbed out of Carlos's car.

"Your picture's in the paper," Stacy said brightly, as if I were just waking up to the news.

"Please move your bike," I said, pointing to the small red-and-white bicycle with slightly lopsided training wheels.

"Your picture's in the paper," she said again.

"I know. Where's Mom?"

Stacy waved toward the kitchen door. I left the girls outside, then opened a cola and wandered back toward my bedroom.

Mom hugged me like we'd been separated for weeks. "Nice job." She picked up the newspaper. "Tell me . . . any more contracts?" She leaned toward me eagerly, hoping for the right answer.

"None," I answered. "How was Cleveland?"

A cloud seemed to come over her, and she looked at the floor a moment before she answered, "Oh, I guess it's okay—it's just not home."

"Make some good contacts today?" Aunt Mof asked.

"Maybe." I handed her the list of businesses where we had stopped. "That last one might be a biggie. Agar Pest Control."

"Why?" they asked, both looking up and speaking at the same time.

"I have an appointment with the big boss in Atlanta tomorrow, 4:30."

I handed Mom the business card. "If you can take me, that is," I said, ready to suggest that we drive Dad's Mustang.

"Hmmmm . . . Tomorrow isn't good," Mom said, shaking her head slowly. "Field trip to Grant Park Zoo with the girls' class. Their teacher is counting on me."

"Take the bus," Aunt Mof said, waving her hand with a motion of finality.

"I don't think I could find the place by myself," I said, with no intention of taking the bus.

"I'm sure Scott and Carlos will go along," Mom said, glad to hear a solution to the problem.

"Well, I don't know."

"Well, of course you can take the bus," Mom said, "and you know Scott and Carlos will go."

She was right. I knew they would go. But I didn't think even the three of us together could find our way around downtown Atlanta, and I didn't want to try.

"Did Dad see the picture?" I asked.

Aunt Mof and Mom exchanged glances, and I didn't need to hear more.

"He saw it," Mom said lightly.

"And he was mad?"

"Oh no, not angry . . . just . . . well, maybe surprised," she said, getting up to leave.

"I'll call the bus station," Aunt Mof said.

"Good. I'll start supper." Mom left the room.

Dad wasn't happy. I knew it.

I got up to follow Mom out, but Aunt Mof stopped me by clearing her throat. I knew it was coming. I'd seen her glance at the cards once or twice while Mom was still talking, and I'd hoped to make a smooth exit before she grabbed me.

"Just ten minutes," she said, as she launched into another half-hour drill.

Aunt Mof had no concept of time. She read off over half the questions in the stack, repeating only two or three that I'd have gotten if she'd given me a few more seconds. I was feeling more prepared for this exam than for any test I'd ever studied for.

At exactly 7 P.M., Mr. Richwine was standing at the door with my badge when Carlos and I rushed into the back of the church. I mumbled my well-worn—and dubious—apology. Sorry. Ushers were expected to be at the church well before 7:00. I could hear Mr. Richwine thinking, but he kept his elastic smile and said nothing. I vowed to myself that tomorrow night we'd be early.

Carlos and I manned the entire pew alone. Scott stayed home to wait for traveling relatives who planned to stop by. The place was more crowded than usual—but only because the usual Wednesday night gathering of adults had come. I didn't see even one new teenager when we walked forward with the cards, or later with the offering plates. I knew Amber wouldn't be there, but I couldn't help looking. Stephanie and Marshall sat near the front on the left side; I served the right side of the aisle.

Later, I sat and held a well-worn and frayed hymnal while my attention drifted. I stared at the dark window and allowed my cluttered thoughts to play across its panes. I couldn't seem to sort out priorities or to see things with a clear perspective. I was sitting with Carlos instead of Amber, I'd suffered intense embarrassment with my picture on the front page of the newspaper, I was scheduled for a useless trip to Atlanta tomorrow to see Mr. Agar, and Mom had already looked at houses in Cleveland.

"Welcome," Pastor Eric said, and my attention jumped to the pulpit. "Turn with me to I Timothy 4:1 and 2."

My Bible was in Carlos's car, but I listened as intently as my wandering mind would allow.

For over half an hour Pastor Eric talked about the seared conscience and Satan's strategy for reaching the hearts of God's people.

"Look at Romans 13:5," Pastor Eric exclaimed. His hands waved in the air.

Wherefore ye must needs be subject, not only for wrath, but also for conscience sake.

"That means," Pastor Eric said very slowly and with deliberate control, "that we do right for the sake of a clean conscience, and not just to escape punishment."

Pastor Eric was fifteen minutes into his notes when it began to slowly dawn on me, like the morning light—*the stolen exam. Maybe I had a seared conscience*. It was becoming easier and easier not to think about it. I was honestly glad not to think about it, but I'd been in church long enough to know to be afraid of a seared conscience. I began to study the back of the seat in front of me, avoiding eye contact with Pastor Eric, as though he could read my mind. My throat constricted a little, and my face burned. I was suddenly aware of how warm and stuffy the building was. I knew God was dealing with me—I knew I'd have to respond.

Carlos aimed a sharp blow to my left ankle, and then, without moving his jaws said, "What's wrong with you?"

I shrugged him off and relaxed some. I'd deal with this revelation later.

The cool evening air felt good when we finally headed for Carlos's car. I'd mostly forgotten my encounter with what was left of my conscience and was only faintly aware that I'd soon be dealing with that still small voice again.

"Time for a burger and fries, no?" Carlos asked, heading for McDonald's.

"Always," I said, absentmindedly checking out the players as we passed the lighted tennis courts.

I saw Scott about the same moment that Carlos jammed the brake to the floor, leaving seat belt indentations across my chest.

"¡Oye, mira eso!" Carlos said in the same tone of disgust that I was feeling.

"Can't believe it," I mumbled. Why hadn't he been in church?

"Hey," Scott called, as he hurried over to the car looking like he was glad to see us.

"Well, Mr. Big Shot," Carlos said, "so you couldn't make it to church!"

The accusation was obviously a slap in the face, taking Scott by surprise and making him defensive. His jaw clinched, and his chin jutted out.

"Well?" Carlos persisted. "You were supposed to have relatives over. I don't see 'em," he said, looking all around in an exaggerated way.

"I don't have to answer your questions!" Scott said in a defensive tone.

"So, what happened?" I finally spoke up as I glanced over at Carlos.

"They came and left within half an hour. Period. No big deal." Scott shrugged, already over his anger. "You've still got time for a couple of games," he said with a nod toward the courts.

"In these clothes?" Carlos said with a snort, still irritated that Scott had played without us.

Scott joined us, and ten minutes later the three of us were putting away French fries and Big Macs.

"How about a trip to Atlanta tomorrow?" I asked casually.

"Agar?" Scott asked.

"Yeah."

"With your mom?"

"No. Just us."

"You driving?" Carlos asked, surprised. None of us had been driving long enough to tackle Atlanta traffic.

"Nope. We'll take the bus."

"The bus." Scott said it with a scowl. I didn't blame him. I didn't like the idea either, and I didn't care if neither of them wanted to go. It would be a good excuse to cancel the appointment.

"I guess so." Scott shrugged.

"Sure," Carlos said.

I hadn't the faintest idea where the place was, but I knew Aunt Mof would have all the details by the time school was out.

I got out of the car, and Carlos pulled away from the curb just as Dad turned into our driveway.

"Well," Dad said in a tone of voice that I couldn't quite identify, "you've been busy while we were gone. Edith had several appointments lined up for me this afternoon. It seems your advertising talents are getting some attention."

I knew he was thinking of the picture in the paper, but he didn't sound mad.

"Yeah," I said, waiting for whatever came next. Dad sat on the steps and motioned for me to sit too. Henrietta joined us.

"Well," he said slowly, "I signed three more small contracts."

"You did?"

"Yes, and well . . . this is wonderful . . . but . . . it's making it more and more difficult to make plans for Cleveland," he said, as if he were searching for the right words.

"Sure, Dad; that's the idea. Enough contracts and we stay. Remember?"

"If enough contracts come in, I'm sure it will be God's provision. And He can certainly work through you boys." Dad studied the sidewalk and ran his hand down Henrietta's back several times, while I swatted mosquitoes and started feeling more and more uncomfortable about this conversation.

"I know what I said." He paused several moments. "And I'm proud of your efforts, son, but . . . " Dad didn't finish. He didn't have to, and I didn't want to hear it.

Mom came to the door, and abruptly the subject was changed.

An hour later I lay staring at the ceiling in the family room.

"What's the use?" I whispered to Henrietta. "Dad's determined to go." For almost twenty minutes I sank deeper and deeper in self-pity, consumed by an almost paralyzing hopelessness. Then, impulsively I sprang up and made my way through the dark house back to my bedroom. As I'd hoped, the light was still on, and the door open.

"What's the use?" I said, startling Aunt Mof as she sat pecking away at her keyboard. "Dad's determined to go."

Recovering from the sudden interruption, Aunt Mof motioned for me to come over and sit, and then for several long moments she said nothing as she took off her reading glasses and rubbed her eyes.

"I know he is," she finally said. "I heard him talking to your mother."

"Then why bother with all this . . . this . . . this . . . bother?" I said, waving at the pages of notes on the bed.

Aunt Mof picked up a sheet of paper and looked at a list of businesses where I had talked to owners or managers and given them Dad's fliers.

"Well," she said slowly, "I don't know what God's will is in this, but I do know that we have prayed and we'll continue to pray. And, like it says in the Bible in Ephesians, *having done all, we'll stand.*"

She smiled. "Don't quit and don't give up. If it's God's will for you to stay here, then He'll change your dad's mind. And, if it's God's will for you to move to Cleveland, you sure don't want to stay here."

I do want to stay here.

"Here are your instructions for tomorrow." Aunt Mof handed me a sheet from the printer. "The bus leaves Miller's Shopping Plaza at 2:30. Can you leave tennis practice early tomorrow?"

"Sure."

"Round trip to Atlanta is $9.00. You have money?"

I nodded as I studied the long page of instructions.

"You may need to grab a cab when you get off at the Peachtree stop, depending on the time," she said. "It's all written down."

I really didn't want to go, and I was dreading the hassle more and more.

"Get some sleep," she said with a sympathetic tone.

At 7:30 the next morning I automatically made my way down the street toward Scott's house. The guys sat on the porch, waiting. I walked on, my mind in Ohio.

"Hello?" Carlos called. "Are you there?"

"No," I answered flatly.

Carlos ignored my mood. "We need to talk about the kids' tennis camp coming up in two weeks. Remember, we promised Coach we'd organize it again this year."

"I'll be in Cleveland by then."

"What?"

"I said I'll be in Cleveland by then."

"No!" Scott said forcefully and launched into a locker room pep talk. "You'll be on the tennis courts with two dozen elementary kids, showing them how to hold their rackets and chasing their wild shots."

I shrugged, unable to shake the depression that continued to weigh me down.

Amber's desk was empty again, and I missed her, but I doubted that even Amber could have cheered me up. The rest of the school day, through lunch and tennis practice, was much the same—lingering depression and a long face that I couldn't seem to prop up.

We left practice early and hurried to Carlos's house to get his car for the three-mile drive to Miller's Plaza.

"Wish I could go with you," Carlos said, as we stood at the bus stop. "Abuelita insists she needs my help today."

I shrugged and heaved another long sigh. His grandmother often needed him. "This trip won't do any good anyway," I said again, as I leaned up against the bench.

"¡Siéntate y cállate!" Carlos exclaimed furiously. "Sit down and be quiet."

My eyebrows shot up, and my jaw dropped a foot. "I don't have to sit, and I don't have to be quiet."

I'd been ready for a confrontation with someone over something for hours.

"*¡Si!* . . . yes . . . yes you do!" Carlos half gasped and half shouted. "You've been whining all day, and I've had enough."

My eyes narrowed and my face burned, but I kept quiet.

"We're going to do all we possibly can to convince your dad to stay here in Cross Springs," he shouted. "That includes going to Atlanta and seeing this Agar guy. Then, right up to the last minute we'll take fliers to every business in the county. After that, if you end up in Cleveland, it'll be because God wants you there. And if that happens, it'll be because that's where you belong."

I was speechless. In the three years I'd known Carlos, I'd never seen that side of him.

"Bus," Scott said.

We watched Carlos get in his car and make a U-turn.

The ride to Atlanta was a little subdued, but I was beginning to have new respect for Carlos. My mood lifted, and by the time we got off the bus at the Peachtree crossing, I was somewhat optimistic about this Mr. Agar. After all, he had invited me, and the lady at the Cross Springs office had said that he liked to support kids in business.

We stood a moment to get our bearings as the bus pulled away, leaving a lung-searing trail of black fumes. We looked at Aunt Mof's sheet of instructions. "Which way?" Scott asked.

I didn't answer, and I didn't move. The four lanes of traffic on both streets at this intersection were bumper to bumper. We needed to be back here by 5:30 if we expected to catch the bus home. We saw no stores in any direction, and every building looked like an office complex of some sort. Most of the buildings had fancy names above the door instead of street numbers. The Haley-Varner Building or the Maxwell Vanderbilt complex.

"Which way?" Scott asked again.

I knew we stayed on Peachtree. "This way," I said, trying to sound confident. I had a fifty-fifty chance of being right. If the next intersection was Piedmont Road, I'd guessed right.

Ten minutes later, after sharing the sidewalk with hundreds of pushy people who thought they owned it, I knew I'd guessed wrong. It was hard to admit.

"We picked the wrong direction." I turned the map around.

"We?"

I shrugged and looked at my watch, beginning to feel the pressure of time. We were supposed to see Mr. Agar at 4:30. We had thirty-five minutes.

"Let's take a taxi," Scott said.

"And put out another nine dollars? Look, it's only eight blocks down Peachtree," I held up the map, counting streets from the X where we got off the bus.

"Well, now it's nine blocks."

"We'll have plenty of time," I said, ignoring his barb about the wrong direction. I folded the map and Aunt Mof's notes and instructions. The map we were using was something Aunt Mof had downloaded from the Internet, and it was hard to judge how long it really was from intersection to intersection.

"I think we should take a taxi," Scott said again after we'd walked two more long blocks and killed another fifteen minutes.

I checked my watch again. "I don't see any taxis." Actually, we had seen a hundred of them flying in both directions, occasionally whipping over to the curb for some experienced passenger to leap in before the wheels quit turning. We walked faster.

Suddenly a taxi pulled to the curb right in front of us, and right away two mafia types with huge briefcases jumped in.

"Come on," I said, starting to run.

The next intersection was Ponce DeLeon, and we were both out of breath by the time we crossed.

I checked my watch again. "Okay, you were right. We should have found a taxi."

"You want a cab?" a strange voice asked.

I struggled for a response as we stood staring at what must have been a resident of the street. He wore two coats—it was warm out—and his shoes were held together with duct tape. We must have hesitated a moment too long, because suddenly he shifted his armload of bags, and with a slight movement of his hand, directed a fast-moving taxi to the curb in front of us.

"Thanks," I mumbled, almost mesmerized by this guy. We climbed into the cab.

"Where to today?" the driver asked, as though he delivered us one place or another regularly.

I leaned up over the seat, shoved Aunt Mof's page of instructions toward him, and showed him the address. He nodded and forced his way in between a new Lincoln and a '65 Mustang. Scott poked me with his elbow and gestured with his chin. We both admired the Mustang.

"You boys sightseeing?" The huge Hispanic cab driver shouted his question over the sound of traffic.

With all four windows down, his dark hair shot in all directions as he waited, looking in our direction for an answer, until I mentally hit the brakes for him.

"We're seeing a client," Scott said over the noise, with a tone that expressed the tension I felt.

"That's good. Real good," he said, turning back around. "You'll do great. Kids should start early in business." He punctuated the air with his hands and never had more than three fingers on the steering wheel at one time. "You'll be rich before you're thirty!"

That was nice to hear, but hard to take seriously.

The cab driver pulled up next to a fire hydrant and turned around with his hand out. "Six bucks." It sounded like more of a challenge than a request.

"Six bucks." I scowled as he shot back into a three-foot opening in traffic.

"Come on," Scott said.

By the time we found the right entrance to the building, the right set of elevators, the right floor, and the right office, we were right late. It was 4:45.

"I'm sorry, sir." The secretary reached over and picked up a green feather from the corner of her desk. "Mr. Agar left just two or three minutes ago. It's his granddaughter's birthday, and he couldn't wait any longer."

I berated myself when we stepped back into the hallway. "Stupid, stupid, stupid. We should have looked for a taxi the minute we got off that bus."

"I've got an idea," Scott murmured. "Come on."

For the next five minutes I hurried to stay on Scott's heels as he rushed down the hallway, down the stairs, and on down to the basement parking garage.

“What?” I called, catching up to him. “What do you think you’re doing?”

“Look.” Scott had a satisfied smile across his face.

With my brows drawn together, I glanced all around the garage. I still didn’t have a clue.

“Mr. Agar?” Scott approached a total stranger.

“Yes.”

“I’m Scott Cunningham.”

“Nice to meet you,” he said, but only because he had to.

“ . . . and this is Mike Prickett.”

Mr. Agar nodded as he looked down with a frustrated sigh at the flat tire on his BMW sports coupé.

“You . . .” he said, “would you mind.” Mr. Agar handed me the birdcage he had been carrying, and for the first time I noticed the green parakeet. Scott had noticed Mr. Agar and his bird when we first entered the building. Good ol’ Scott. He saw the green feather on the secretary’s desk and put two and two together.

“Let me get that,” Scott said helpfully, taking the jack from Mr. Agar’s hands and then reaching for the spare tire.

I shifted the birdcage from one hand to the other, wondering why he hadn’t just set it on the garage floor or put it in the still-locked car.

Then I caught Scott’s expression—narrowed eyes and slight jerk of his head toward Mr. Agar. I cleared my throat and prepared to launch my well-practiced spiel.

“Mr. Agar,” I said, talking loudly and somewhat animated. “I just missed an appointment with you, and I apologize for being late.”

His expression changed slightly. I think he suddenly placed who I was—the kid in the newspaper. “Oh, oh yes,” he said briskly and shoved his hand toward me.

I shifted the cage again, and we shook. Then, smoothing out the slightly wrinkled copy of the flier, I handed it to him and began. While Scott changed the tire, I went over the flier, then talked in detail about Dad's talents, and reputation, and experience. Mr. Agar was such a good listener, nodding at the right times and making positive noises now and then, that I got carried away. Suddenly I saw Scott raise his thumb to his neck and make a sudden slice motion. Cut.

I finished quickly. "Mr. Agar, I understand that you are very active in the Junior Chamber of Commerce and might be interested in supporting young people in business."

He brightened noticeably at the mention of the Junior Chamber of Commerce.

"Oh, yes. I firmly support the JCC," he said. He put the jack back in the trunk and opened his car door. "Thanks very much, Scott. I'd like to talk to you, boys," he said, taking the parakeet, "but I'm expected at a birthday party in Forsyth, and I'm running late.

"Forsyth?" Scott asked. "Then you must go right past the Cross Springs exit."

"Well, uh, yes," Mr. Agar said.

Boldly, Scott went on. "Any chance we could hitch a ride to that exit? I think we're about to miss our bus."

I held my breath and looked at Mr. Agar for a few seconds while he weighed this request.

"Well, I don't see why not. Sure. Jump in."

There was no jumping in. Scott and I both had to fold up like accordions to fit inside the small car. I sat up front and let the seat slide back a few inches to get my knees down below my chin. Mr. Agar passed the parakeet to Scott. Scott's hulklike frame seemed to fill the entire back seat. I glanced back and snickered a little as Scott brushed birdseed off his pants. Then, I put on a confident, businesslike expression, prepared to ask Mr. Agar if Dad could call him.

"I'm glad you asked about the JCC," he said, sliding easily into the driver's seat.

I didn't remember asking about it.

"The organization was formed back in 1915 in St. Louis. At that time it was called the Young Men's Progressive Civic Association."

Mr. Agar left the parking garage like a taxi driver and talked about the JCC without taking a breath for another fifteen minutes. "We stress leadership training and civic involvement for young people just your age. If Cross Springs doesn't have a local group, we need to start one."

At that moment, I wasn't the least bit interested.

"We're already active in over seventy-five countries," he said proudly, as though he had personally been involved in them all.

I turned slightly and shot Scott a helpless expression and an almost imperceptible shrug. Scott rolled his eyes. There was simply no polite way to interrupt and change the subject.

After almost an hour-long monologue, the car pulled off at the Cross Springs exit and stopped at an Exxon station. "Got far to walk, boys?"

"No, sir. Thanks for the ride, Mr. Agar," I said, picking up the flier and continuing without a pause, "Prickett Small Business Consulting can help with all of your financial decisions, and I'd like your permission to tell my dad that Agar Pest Control is interested in more information." Then I paused, waiting for some indication of his interest.

"Mike." Mr. Agar smiled and gestured widely with both palms up. "I decided yesterday morning when I saw your picture in the paper that I wanted to do business with Prickett. It just so happens that you caught me at a perfect time. I'll call your dad tomorrow."

I was dumbfounded. "That'll be great," I finally said in a feeble voice.

We stood calmly as the BMW left the station and made its way back up the ramp to the interstate. Then Scott and I both let out whoops and assaulted the air with punches of victory and success.

We shook hands violently and almost skipped all the way home. Scott cut off for home a block before I did. We had only about forty minutes before Carlos would be picking us up for the youth rally.

From the sky to the pit—my exhilaration hit the dirt like a meteor when I neared our driveway. There, planted next to the ivy-covered mailbox, was a big red, white, and blue For Sale sign. I froze on the sidewalk, and then glanced around, thinking I was at the wrong house. It was home all right, but it wouldn't be for long. Within seconds my face turned a clammy cold that moved down to my toes. Then, a wave of despair flushed over me.

I opened the back door deliberately and with considerable control. Mom wiped her red eyes, and Dad pushed back from the table.

"You're home," Mom said, smiling a little.

I nodded, avoided Dad, and moved toward the hallway and my bedroom. Aunt Mof would give me straight answers.

"Mike," Dad said, "I had hoped we could talk before the sign went up."

I shrugged.

"Did you make progress in Atlanta?" Mom asked hopefully.

"Maybe," I said casually.

Dad straightened his shoulders and raised his chin. "Can we talk?"

"Dad, I need to get ready for church," I said, then I stood in the doorway without looking at him, waiting for a sign that I could move on.

"All right then," he said, "we'll talk later."

I burst into my room through the open door, arms waving, control lost. "There's a For Sale sign in our front yard."

"I know," Aunt Mof said quietly.

"Dad intends to move to Cleveland."

"I know."

"He doesn't care how I feel."

"I guess it seems that way," Aunt Mof said sympathetically.

"He promised. He promised we'd stay if we got five good contracts."

"I know," Aunt Mof said and gave a helpless shrug. "What happened in Atlanta today?"

I couldn't generate even a flicker of enthusiasm as I told her about Mr. Agar and his twenty-one Pest Control offices around central Georgia.

"You mean he's ready to sign a contract? Just like that?"

"That's what he said." I flipped on the computer to check my e-mail.

"Why, Michael," Aunt Mof exclaimed with renewed enthusiasm, "that's wonderful."

It seemed wonderful half an hour ago, but now it didn't seem to matter. "I guess," I said, heaving a sigh.

"Well . . . " she said slowly, "I'll say it again. I don't know what God's will is in this, but like it says in Ephesians, *having done all, we'll stand*. And Michael, right now we haven't done all. It's not standing time yet—there is still time to work, time to pass out fliers, time to talk to prospects, and time to make phone calls. Why, who knows, your dad may come in tomorrow with Mr. Agar's business—that sounds like two significant contracts to me—and yank up that sign out front."

The pep talk ended just as I logged onto the Internet and heard the familiar recorded voice say, "you have mail." There were a dozen messages, but only one caught my attention. AMBERDELL. "She's back," I murmured with more enthusiasm than I thought was left in me. Her message was short. Only four words. "Let's try again tonight."

I checked my watch and hurried down the hall. I had ten minutes to clean up and change clothes.

I walked past the newly planted sign and got in the back seat of Carlos's car. I tried to ignore his and Scott's surprised expressions, and remembering Carlos's earlier tongue-lashing, I said nothing. I was determined not to whine, so I couldn't think of anything to say. None of us could think of anything to say.

Finally, Carlos spoke up and stated the obvious, "Your dad's determined to move, isn't he?"

With a lump in my throat the size of a grapefruit, I could only nod *yes.*

We made it to church on time for a change, and I stood in a daze while Mr. Richwine pinned my badge to my shirt. *We're really moving to Cleveland.* The thought kept coming.

"Mike." Scott called softly from the double doors, and I followed him to our seats. Carlos held the hymnal, and I stared at the page. *We're really moving to Cleveland.* A sharp blow to my ankle several minutes later prompted me to bow my head during the prayer, but I didn't hear the words. I had too many things to think about.

"You're up," Scott whispered, and I moved to join the rest of the ushers. I was thankful someone was telling me what to do.

When we passed the collection plates, I saw Amber for the first time in the twenty minutes I'd been in the church. She had saved me a seat, and I looked forward to sitting next to her.

"Turn with me to Matthew 24:40," Pastor Eric said as he turned the pages of his Bible.

Amber found the reference right away, while I stared at my Bible.

Pastor Eric began a message on the Rapture and end times, while I struggled to focus on the here and now.

I suddenly noticed the toe of Amber's shoe. It bounced very slightly to the tune of an imagined song, and I watched for a moment before my attention snapped back to Pastor Eric's voice.

In a moment, in the twinkling of an eye, at the last trump: for the trumpet shall sound, and the dead shall be raised incorruptible . . . I Corinthians 15:52.

I tried to listen to the message, but moments later I found myself staring at the hymnal in the slot in front of me. Dad promised. He promised, and now he's not even giving us a chance.

"If your heart's not right, you're not ready," Pastor Eric boomed, drawing my attention back to the pulpit. Then he began to describe an experience he'd had with a new convert on a mission trip to Mexico, but before he got to the end, I was gone again.

If Mom tried harder, I'll bet she could talk him out of it, I thought.

For forty minutes Pastor Eric spoke, and I alternately listened and daydreamed—and then raced to catch up with him again. Even being near Amber didn't make my heart flutter like it usually did.

After the altar call and the closing hymn, we stood and I followed Amber into the aisle.

"Are you okay?" she asked, her eyebrows drawn together in concern.

Everything in me wanted to pour out my troubles to her. I needed sympathy, but I was determined not to whine. "I guess I have a lot on my mind," I said, ready to ask her to go to McDonald's with us.

"Well, I need to rush—my dad will be out front waiting."

And poof—she was gone. I'd sat by Amber for forty-five minutes and dreamed away most of those minutes. I sighed again.

"Let's go," Scott said, taking my badge and tossing it to Mr. Richwine.

I followed obediently.

"Want to go to McDonald's?" Carlos asked.

Not without Amber, I thought.

"Not without money," Scott said, after checking his pockets.

We headed back to my house and a conference with Aunt Mof.

We walked back to my room and found Aunt Mof on the phone. She sat propped up on the bed with the big casts on her legs covered by a bright blue and white striped sheet.

"Any more contracts?" Scott asked when she finally hung up.

"Actually, yes. That was Edith," Aunt Mof said brightly, gesturing to the phone. "Your dad got two more small contracts today. Edith sounded excited about it." Aunt Mof tapped the pencil eraser on her chin and appeared to be thinking. "He hasn't said a word about it, but Edith tells me that makes a total of nine small contracts already—mostly from the fliers—and mostly since the clown picture."

The four of us looked at each other, wondering what effect all this might have on Dad. Aunt Mof smiled and reached for the well-worn stack of cards.

This is overkill, I thought.

"Uh, I think we know all those already," Scott said, taking a step back.

"Oh you do? To which country does "The Great Leap Forward" apply? With which country would one associate the Red Guard? What country controlled Vietnam prior to 1954?"

She really didn't give him time to answer, but those were the three questions that Scott kept getting confused over yesterday.

"Well . . . maybe a short review," Scott said.

After almost an hour of loud, enthusiastic questions and answers, we escaped to the kitchen. We knew the cards—all the cards. But Aunt Mof would continue to drill until the exam. I really didn't mind.

"Oh, you're home." Dad said.

I'd been home over an hour, but I just nodded.

"Seeya," Carlos called as both guys headed out the back door.

"Did you know," Dad said abruptly, "that Cleveland is the largest city in Ohio."

I didn't care.

"It's right on Lake Erie. Maybe you and I can go fishing there."

I didn't care, and I wasn't interested in fishing . . . but I could tell that Dad was trying—and that did soften my mood some.

"The Cuyahoga River runs near the city."

I heaved a long, silent sigh.

"Well, I'm sorry," Dad finally said after an awkward pause. "I know this is hard for you."

He whacked me on the shoulder with an affectionate blow and sat down at the table with his newspaper.

I tried to think of a way to tell Dad all that was going on, but I just didn't have it in me. Maybe later.

After Dad turned the kitchen light off I lay next to Henrietta, staring up at the dark ceiling. "If you're not right, you're not ready," Pastor Eric had said. I thought about the stolen exam and my seared conscience. I hadn't let myself think about the exam in a couple of days. I doubted that I could really be right with God until that was settled.

If we confess our sins, he is faithful and just to forgive us our sins, and to cleanse us from all unrighteousness. I didn't doubt for one second that God would forgive if I was sincere, and I was—but I wasn't looking forward to taking the consequences. And I wasn't ready to deal with all the issues bombarding my mind. I just wanted to sleep.

. . . for I have learned, in whatsoever state I am, therewith to be content.

The thoughts kept coming. I knew the scripture wasn't referring to Ohio, or even California or Mississippi, but it seemed appropriate somehow.

I nudged Henrietta to the floor and walked to the back door. We both went out, and I quietly closed the door and sat on the steps. There was no moon and the sky was black. The street light in front of the house next door pitched shadows across the yard, and a cool breeze ruffled my hair.

I sat almost fifteen minutes, sorting my thoughts and stroking Henrietta's curly ears.

Finally, with a deliberate act of my will, I gave in. "Lord," I said, feeling clumsy but confident in what I was saying, "I know you want me to confess my part in the stolen exam . . . and I should have already done it. And if You want me in Cleveland, then that's where I want to be." Once I'd said it—and I meant it—I was flooded with relief.

After sitting in the cool darkness several minutes longer, I thought of Aunt Mof's words earlier in the day. It's not standing time yet—there is still time to work, time to pass out fliers, time to talk to prospects, time to make phone calls. Yes. I would do all that. But suddenly, I wasn't frantically fearful of moving to Cleveland.

Chapter 11

"Kids' tennis camp ready?" Coach asked as we left the courts Friday afternoon.

"Same as last year. We just changed the dates," Scott answered.

"Got your coaches lined up?"

"Same as last year. The three of us, and Dustin, Arney, and Mark."

"Put the notices on the bulletin boards around the elementary school?"

"Doing that today," Carlos said, as if the signs were all made up and in the back seat of his car.

"Good job. See ya' on Monday," Coach said as he fished his car keys from his pocket.

Within ten minutes we were in the fifth-grade classroom asking Miss Eldridge for paper and markers to whip up our signs.

"May we please borrow some thumbtacks?" Scott asked, as polite as I've ever seen him.

By 4 P.M. we were rearranging TVs and VCRs. We put the repaired ones on higher shelves and brought down equipment that was ready for repair. Then, while Scott washed the front windows, Carlos and I swept the aisles.

"Howz business, Eddie?"

"Better than it's been in a long time."

"Good. That's real good."

"Been handing out your fliers when customers come in here."

"Oh yeah?"

"Yeah. And some lady came in this morning wanting a phone number for the clown."

"Why?" I said, suddenly pausing to look up.

"Needs a clown for her kid's birthday party," Eddie said with a slight grin.

"Well, I hope you didn't give her my number," I said indignantly, insulted at the thought.

"Pays real good."

"I don't care."

"Fifty dollars for an hour and a half."

Now *that* was tempting, and I paused before I said resolutely, "Not interested."

Eddie shrugged.

"You're nuts," Scott said. "I'll do it for fifty dollars."

I knew he wouldn't.

Carlos pulled up at four more businesses on the way home, and I spent several minutes at each place talking to the owner or manager. Two of them mentioned the picture in the newspaper. One just smiled that telltale smile. I wrote down the names of the places and the excuses each one gave. Aunt Mof would take it from there.

"Thanks," I said, getting out of the car in front of my house. Carlos had dropped Scott off first. He'd be back in an hour to pick me up for the last night at the youth rally. I looked forward to sitting with Amber again. Last night I'd been neck-deep in despair. I must have been pretty sorry company.

Both cars were gone. I knew Mom and Dad were away. I popped the tab on a soda and went back to check my e-mail.

"Aunt Mof?" I called, more than a little surprised to find the room empty.

"Aunt Mof?" I called louder.

I walked back to the other end of our large L-shaped house.

"Aunt Mof?" I said more quietly—hesitating—aware that she was definitely not in the house.

I stood a moment, my mind a little disoriented. She had to be here.

Back in her room, I flipped on my computer and then stood looking around, thinking. Her nightgown and robe were on the floor next to the bed. Aunt Mof wasn't the neatest guest we'd ever had.

Suddenly last night's Scripture popped into my mind. *Then shall two be in the field; the one shall be taken, and the other left*—The Rapture.

After about two soul-searching seconds, I relaxed. Mike, I thought, with a big dumb grin, you must be a few clowns short of a circus. "They're not gone," I said out loud. "If they were, I'd be gone too. I'm ready. For three years I've been ready."

I still didn't have a clue where Aunt Mof might be, but I checked my e-mail, and after deleting a few advertisements, signed off the Internet, and headed for the shower.

"Mikey's home," Miranda shrieked twenty minutes later, and it was a relief to hear her voice.

"Aunt Mof got new things on her legs," Stacy said in her high-pitched, shrill voice.

"She got what?"

"Walking casts," Aunt Mof said, as Mom helped her up the steps and into the waiting wheelchair. "I can't walk much, though," she said, breathing hard. "Not with both legs so weak."

Carlos honked the horn, and I picked up my Bible on the way out the door.

After the music and the offering, I slid easily into the seat next to Amber. I looked over at her, enjoying her perfume and admiring her long brown hair. After the half hour on the back steps last night, I was a different person—relaxed and ready to hear what Pastor Eric had to say.

"Obedience is better than sacrifice," Pastor Eric boomed.

Behold, I set before you this day a blessing and a curse; A blessing, if ye obey the commandments of the LORD your God, which I command you this day: And a curse, if ye will not obey the commandments of the LORD.

"That's Deuteronomy 11:26-28," he said. "Obedience is better than sacrifice."

I didn't really apply that Scripture to myself, but I found it easy to listen tonight. Then Pastor Eric talked for several minutes on what a blessing and a curse should mean to us as teenagers.

"Obedience results in blessings," Pastor Eric said with conviction.

I crossed and uncrossed my legs and struggled to avoid the impact of the Scripture I kept hearing. The stolen exam had become hot again and burned in my consciousness. It demanded that I deal with it. I had promised God that I'd confess my part in the mess, and it was time to start talking. Time to obey. Suddenly I knew what I needed to do. I would not take the history final before I admitted my guilt, even though I might not be allowed to take the exam after that. Those thoughts came this time without stress or fear.

Later, two hundred teens filled the aisles and drifted toward the foyer of the building.

"Uh, Amber," I said in a somewhat strained voice, dreading rejection, "do you have time for pizza at my house?"

She paused for less than a second before answering, "I'll ask my dad."

"I can drive you home later," I said, hoping that Dad and his Mustang would be home.

We walked out to the street where her dad waited, trying to read a newspaper by the glow of the dome light.

"Hi, Mr. Dellaney," I said in a slightly high-pitched voice. I'd spoken to him several times in the past, but never under these circumstances.

"Daddy, Mike invited me to his house for pizza. Okay if I go? He can bring me home later."

"Is it okay with your parents, Mike?" Mr. Dellaney said.

"Oh, yes, sir!"

He shrugged and folded his newspaper. "Can you have her home before ten?"

That gave us an hour and a half. I wasn't sure I could come up with an hour and a half's worth of conversation, but I was willing to try.

"Yes, sir!"

"Mom, Aunt Mof, this is Amber." I watched their surprised expressions.

"Hello," Amber said shyly with a friendly smile.

Stacy and Miranda came in to inspect the guest.

In the next fifteen minutes we baked pizzas, searched for paper plates, set out glasses and ice, and laughed a lot. It was great, but I found myself wishing Scott and Carlos would take off.

"Have a seat, Amber," Scott said in a real friendly voice as he pulled out a kitchen chair.

I'd have thought of that in a moment.

Carlos handed her a soda and made me feel like an inconsiderate klutz.

Aunt Mof and Mom were back in my bedroom, and the girls were watching a video while we ate pizza and talked about school and the upcoming three-week break.

"Your family planning a vacation?" Scott asked Amber, making me even more annoyed with him.

"Yes, up to North Carolina for a week in the mountains," she answered, seeming to enjoy his attention.

The guys were monopolizing her time and attention, and I was beginning to feel frustrated.

"So, how was the last service of the week?" Mom asked when we joined her and Aunt Mof in my back room.

"It was good. Pastor Eric talked about obedience," Amber said.

Aunt Mof reached for the history cards but froze when she saw my eyebrows shoot up and draw together, while my head gave a slight shake to the side.

She withdrew her hand, and I relaxed.

"I guess you've been working hard getting ready for finals too," Aunt Mof said to Amber.

"Oh yes," she answered, and for the next fifteen minutes Amber chatted easily with Mom and Aunt Mof. I watched the clock, knowing the only time I'd have alone with her was the ten-minute drive to her house. And dad wasn't home with the Mustang. Scott and Carlos occupied themselves on my computer. You can do that at home, I silently shouted at them.

Finally, Amber remembered I was still in the room. "I'd love to see your tennis trophies," she said.

"Sure, come on." I was glad to get her away from the trivial chatter.

"Mikey has hundreds of trophies," Miranda said proudly.

Stacy climbed up on a chair and carefully took down the latest one and handed it to Amber. "This is our new one."

Amber turned the little statue over and over in her hands, admired the gold color, and made some other appropriate comments before she sat down on the sofa. Before I could move, Miranda and Stacy sat—on either side of Amber. This evening was definitely not turning out like I had hoped. The twins were as skilled in idle chitchat as Mom and Aunt Mof. I paced, trying to think of an errand to send them on. Nothing came to mind.

"Mike," Amber said at last, "this has been fun, but it's getting late."

Ahhh, I thought, just what I've been waiting for. "I'll get the car keys."

"Carlos, I need your car for about twenty minutes," I said. There was no way I'd take my girl home in the pink eyesore, and Dad was still at the office.

"Why?" he asked, starting to stand.

"Just gimme the keys."

Carlos tossed the keys in my direction and then slumped back down in the chair in front of my computer. Aunt Mof never looked up from her magazine.

"Ready?" I smiled and cocked my head slightly to one side in a casual pose, ready to take back some control.

"Can we go, Mikey?" Miranda asked in a cheery voice, as she headed for the car.

"NO."

"Oh, Mike, let them come along," Amber said in a pleading tone. "They're so cute."

Right now I couldn't think of Stacy and Miranda as *cute.* They were pests. And they were in the car before I could think of a response. I forced a smile and a shrug.

We were back in fifteen minutes, and the twins had monopolized every minute of the ride to and from Amber's house.

"Go to bed," I growled.

"But Mom said we—"

"GO TO BED NOW," I ordered with a glare. I left the kitchen wondering why I was so disagreeable around the girls lately.

"Here," I said and tossed Carlos his keys. He signed off the Internet and turned off the computer.

I fell into a chair and let my sour expression darken the room.

"What's your problem?" Scott asked, oblivious.

"Well, if you can't figure it out, I'm not saying." First Scott and Carlos, then Mom and Aunt Mof, and then Miranda and Stacy had occupied every minute of the hour and a half I could have had with Amber.

Aunt Mof ignored my outburst, picked up her stack of cards, and kicked off another review session. I was over my pout half an hour later when Aunt Mof abruptly put down the cards and said, "Have you boys had that talk with Mrs. Valbueno and Mr. Fielder yet?" She knew we hadn't.

I picked at my fingernails, and Scott and Carlos seemed to focus on their shoes.

"Ummmm," she murmured and nodded as she picked up her Bible. "Well, of course our standing with God is based on the work of His Son for us, not on what we do or don't do, but God does expect obedience. Maybe we should talk about your standing with God."

It was getting warm and stuffy in the room.

"What *is* a Christian?" she asked.

"Someone who prays."

"Someone who goes to church."

"Someone who repents."

Aunt Mof shook her head, "I didn't ask what a Christian does. I asked what a Christian *is*."

We must have looked blankly at her.

"Okay, what if I said, 'What is a millionaire?' "

"Someone who has a million bucks," Carlos answered.

"Right. So, what *is* a Christian?"

"Someone who has Jesus Christ," Carlos answered again.

"You got it." Aunt Mof said with a big smile.

Then she told us about her experience of salvation and went on to ask a lot of questions about our experiences with God. I was sure of my own salvation, but after half an hour or so, I also felt confident of Scott's and Carlos's salvation. They had been having the same problems I'd been having. We were inconsistent in our walk with God.

"Do you know what Satan's biggest lie is?" Aunt Mof asked.

We sat like statues.

"He loves to convince Christians to wait. Linger, pause, delay—just put off whatever God says to do."

Aunt Mof put aside her Bible and abruptly changed the subject. "I have some good news."

We waited expectantly while she paused a moment before going on.

"And the good news is . . . ?" I asked.

"Your dad signed three more contracts today—all because of the fliers and the picture in the paper."

We pitched a celebration with pats on the back and loud congratulations to each other.

"Is any of this making a dent in Dad's plans?" I asked, daring to hope.

"I don't know." Aunt Mof shrugged. "But you might as well know the bad news too."

"Bad news?" Our celebrating came to a halt.

"When Edith said Mr. Agar hadn't called by 5:00 as he had said he would, I called his office and talked with him myself." Aunt Mof watched for our reactions.

Agar Pest Control was a biggie—twenty-one offices—and I considered that contract almost a done deal, the one possibility that might keep Dad here.

"It seems that he mentioned the deal to his wife, who reminded him that his nephew was in some kind of financial consulting business. He was very sorry, but he'd have to stick with the family."

Scott sat down and let out a sound like a moan as his head hung down toward his knees, and his hands roughly massaged the top of his head.

Carlos heaved a sigh and slammed his fist to his palm. *"¡No es justo!"*

Both of them looked over at me. The verse from Psalms was playing over in my mind: . . . *But the salvation of the righteous is of the LORD: he is their strength in the time of trouble.*

They didn't understand why I didn't react. I didn't understand it either. Aunt Mof just smiled.

"One more possibility," she said. "I made an appointment for you right after school Monday, boys. Brinkley Insurance. It's a big three-story brick building about five miles south of town. I overheard someone at the doctor's office say that Brinkley Insurance just gave up a huge financial consulting contract. I don't know anything about them. There may be nothing to it, or it could be the biggest one yet."

Early Saturday morning Mom found me struggling with the lawn mower.

"Mike," she said, looking at the sign out by the mailbox, "the real estate people just called. They want to bring a family over to see the house in a little while."

"Well great. That's just great. They can't wait to see us go. Out with the old and in with the new," I said, with a wide sweep of my greasy hand.

"Well," she said sympathetically, "I don't like it either."

I knew she didn't. I'd seen her red eyes several times, and I'd seen her take a Kleenex and leave the room.

I heaved a sigh and turned back to my mower.

I was putting away the mower an hour later when a shiny black Towne Car pulled into the driveway.

A tall gray-haired guy climbed out of the driver's seat and stood next to the car. He was dressed like he was on his way to church—or maybe to a funeral. He introduced himself—Fred something.

"Your folks home?" he asked and then handed me his business card.

"I'll go see," I said, trying to sound annoyed at the inconvenience.

Mom came out, and he introduced himself again, and then introduced the couple and their loud kids. I went looking for Aunt Mof.

"They just couldn't wait. That sign hasn't been in the yard forty-eight hours and here comes the parade."

"What are your plans for the day?" Aunt Mof asked.

I spread the slats in the miniblinds and looked out over the back yard. "We're working for Eddie. Those kids are in Mom's flower beds."

"Eddie's business must be improving?" she asked and stated at the same time.

"He's doing real well. Would you look at that—they're climbing my tree. That's my tree house."

"Oh? How long has it been since you were up in that tree house?"

I ignored the question. We both knew it had been several years. I could hear the muffled voices of the intruders in the kitchen and Mom's voice as she said, "Just take your time and look around."

After standing near the door listening for several minutes, I turned to Aunt Mof when I heard them in the hallway.

"Did the rats in the attic bother you last night?"

"What?"

"Wow, what a huge room!" Mrs. Intruder exclaimed as she came in, obviously in love with the place.

They examined the room like a white-glove inspection. They looked in the closet and bathroom and measured the built-in bookcases. I'm taking those with me, I thought.

"The plumbing is working today," I said helpfully.

"You must hate to leave this place," Fred Somebody said in a real patronizing tone as the whole bunch of them moved back to the hall.

"Did they see the crack in the wall?" I said loudly to no one in particular as soon as I half closed the door.

Aunt Mof just frowned. "Rats? And a crack in the wall? Really, Michael!"

I gave a helpless, shoulder-lifting, palms-up shrug. It was a mean thing to do, I decided as I watched out the window again. Although I had dealt with the move . . . it was still hard seeing people examine the house.

I took Fred's business card out of my pocket, ripped it up, and threw it in the direction of the trash can. "I'm going to Eddie's," I said, tired of waiting for Carlos.

Carlos pulled into Scott's driveway just as I hit the front porch.

"What took you?" I growled.

"What's your problem?" Carlos sounded like he was ready to launch into another lecture.

"Nothing. My house is just full of people wanting to move in, that's all."

Carlos heaved a deep sigh, as his shoulders slumped. "That's rough. I'm sorry."

That's all I needed. A little sympathy. "Yeah, well, I'm not gonna cry about it."

Fifteen minutes later, Eddie met us at his door. "Great news," he said, all smiles.

"You won the lottery?" Scott asked kiddingly.

"I sold seven TVs and VCRs."

"That's great." It really was good news.

"You boys think you can deliver 'em and set 'em up?"

"Sure. Where to?"

"Perkin's Nursing Home over on Salem Street."

"No problem."

"Uhh . . ." he paused. "There's just one catch." Eddie looked at me and then scratched his chin as he lowered his voice and said, "I sort of promised that the clown would entertain the residents there."

"YOU DID WHAT?"

"I'm sorry, Mike. I couldn't help it. She kept talking about the picture in the paper, and somehow it just came out. I didn't think I was going to get the order."

"No way."

Eddie's head drooped, and Scott and Carlos were all over me. "Just once more," they pleaded.

"Look, I probably still have clown white in my eyebrows."

"So? What's the big deal?" Scott said and shrugged.

We hauled the equipment to the nursing home and set up TVs and VCRs in seven of the rooms. No one mentioned the clown, but I had an idea that I'd work on later.

After we swept the aisles and rearranged the workload again for Eddie, we left for a couple of pickups of broken equipment and then headed for the tennis courts. Two hours of hard play felt great.

After dinner Saturday evening I looked for the right moment to get out of the mess Eddie had gotten me into. I approached Mom deliberately. "Do you remember when you dressed up like a clown for the twins' birthday party?"

She eyed me suspiciously, nodding.

"Well, have you ever thought about dressing up and maybe cheering up old people—you know, like at Perkin's Nursing Home?"

"No."

She stood, waiting—not asking any questions—and generally making it harder for me.

"Well, would you?"

"Would I what?"

"Consider clowning at the nursing home, just for half an hour or so. Nothing to it."

"Mike, what's this all about?" she finally asked.

I spent the next ten minutes explaining how it happened that Eddie had volunteered me to put on the makeup and costume again.

"Ummmm . . . " she hummed and started to laugh. "I think entertaining the nursing home residents would be a good experience for you."

I didn't see anything funny about it, but it was useless to beg or argue with her. Another failed plan. One day soon I'd probably be wearing the big red nose again. I'd deal with it.

Chapter 12

Monday morning, three days before the history final exam, we sat waiting for Mrs. Valbueno to arrive and start the review. Instead, Mrs. Schulgen, a substitute teacher, armed with books and briefcase, hurried into the room.

"Mrs. Valbueno is at the hospital with her husband," she explained, as she spread out her load. "We expect her to be away two or three days. I'll be helping you prepare for the final."

I wondered if I'd even be allowed to take the final. I glanced over at Amber and watched her twirl a strand of her long brown hair around her fingers. I sat mesmerized for several moments until Mrs. Schulgen's voice brought me back to reality.

"So, we'll go quickly around the room answering questions. There are a lot of them to cover in an hour."

For the next fifty-five minutes Mrs. Schulgen read off questions over and over, and went up and down the rows of students waiting for answers. A wrong answer or a pause over ten seconds had her going to the next in line. I sat back and tried to look bored, but it was hard not to shout out an answer like the spirited reviews we had so often with Aunt Mof. I noticed that Scott also had to restrain himself. A couple of times I noticed his arm flinch in an effort to keep from lunging forward with his hand in the air. With ten seconds to think, I knew every answer. All three of us knew the answers.

At noon Scott and I sat on the bench under our favorite tree in the courtyard when Carlos came out and handed us our drinks. He smelled like peppermint.

"I . . . uh . . . hope this won't be a problem for you," I said slowly, just as I had rehearsed it, "but I'm not going to take the history final till I've talked to Mr. Fielder and Mrs. Valbueno and confessed my part in the stolen exam." I deliberately stared at my drink as I popped the top and waited for a response. We all knew that once I confessed to my part, they were automatically involved.

"I'll go with you," Scott said after a long pause.

Carlos nodded. He'd go too.

Brinkley Insurance has one of the largest buildings in the county and dozens of cars in the parking lot. Carlos drove around the place a couple of times looking for the main entrance, while I took out a flier and mentally repeated my pitch. I'd been over it dozens of times, but not often at a place like this, and not often at a prearranged appointment. I was nervous. I was always nervous, even though I'd had only two or three grouchy reactions in all the contacts I'd made.

"Try that door," Carlos said.

I took a deep breath, arranged my plastic smile, and climbed the steps to the main entrance. Green plants hung from the high ceiling in the lobby, and several fancy sofas and armchairs covered bright red carpet. It was showy and rich looking. Employees walked from private doors to the elevators and to other private doors—some shuffled through important looking papers and carried fat briefcases. I was about to retreat to Carlos's car when a lady behind a desk cleared her throat and got my attention.

"May I help you?"

"Uh . . ." I stammered, looking at my notes as if I'd forgotten who I was there to see. "I have an appointment with Mr. Brinkley."

"Which one?"

"Which one?" I repeated.

"Senior or junior?"

"Well . . . uh . . ."

"That's okay. Probably junior," she said, picking up the phone. "And your name?"

I told her, and she called upstairs for Junior Brinkley while I turned and made sure Carlos's car was still waiting.

"Mr. Brinkley is on the third floor, and he's expecting you," she said, pointing toward the elevator.

According to the date on a plaque outside the elevator, the Brinkley Building was almost a hundred years old, but it looked like it had been remodeled and decorated yesterday.

The first thing I noticed when I stepped out on the third floor was that the furniture and decorations were almost the same as those downstairs in the lobby—new and fancy. Secretaries looked busy behind the counter. I could see at least four doors opening to the lobby and a hallway with other doors. I stood and took it all in while I waited to be noticed.

"May I help you?" one of the secretaries asked.

"Mike Prickett, here to see Mr. Brinkley," I announced with what I hoped sounded like confidence.

"He'll be with you in a few minutes," she said, gesturing with a glittering hand to a chair near the corner.

I sat.

"I'll lose my house." I overheard the trembling voice of an elderly lady who stood pleading at the other end of a long counter. She has to be older than my grandmother, I thought as I watched her grip her walking cane and lean toward the counter.

"I'm sorry, Mrs. Jackson, but that's just not our responsibility. You didn't understand the terms of the contract." I watched as the man she talked to came around the counter, took her arm, and slowly escorted her to the elevator. Before I could react to her problem, my attention was drawn to a young couple who were leaving an office across the hall. The girl was crying and the guy, probably her husband, was trying to calm her. I couldn't make out all they were saying, but I got the idea that the insurance company was the problem.

I was feeling more and more uncomfortable by the time I heard my name.

"Mr. Prickett?" A man about Dad's age offered his hand. He shook with an intense grip. "I'm Harold Brinkley. Come on back." He walked toward one of the four offices behind the secretaries' desks. Mr. Brinkley looked as flashy as the chandelier, with an artificial smile that beat my own. If he was expecting an older Mr. Prickett, he didn't let it show.

"Have a seat." He waved in the direction of two huge overstuffed wing chairs.

I sank into one of the chairs, took the flier out of a folder, and opened my mouth to launch my well-rehearsed speech.

"So, you're the clown," he said. My phony smile faded, and my shoulders slumped as I slipped the flier back into the folder.

"Prickett Small Business Consulting has numerous ways to improve your business," I said, recovering from the indignity. "As big as this company is," I said, waving from wall to wall, "all the same financial principles apply." I'd read that line in Dad's ad in the Yellow Pages.

"My father started this business almost sixty years ago," he said, changing the subject back to Brinkley.

"Prickett Consulting can help Brinkley Insurance become the best-known, most financially secure insurance company in central Georgia," I said, returning his volley and implying that it currently wasn't the best known.

He took the hit gracefully, stopped talking, and aimed a skinny finger at me.

"Right—so tell me about your biz!"

I cautiously removed the flier again and made sure I had the floor this time. Then I handed him the paper and deliberately went over every item. I explained in detail things that seemed to catch his attention. As usual, I ended the monologue with, "And so, Mr. Brinkley, may I tell my dad that Brinkley Insurance is interested in finding out more about Prickett Small Business Consulting?"

Mr. Brinkley leaned back and crossed his arms, then looked at me several long moments. He moved his head slightly back and focused over his nose. "As a matter of fact," he said slowly, "you'd have no way of knowing this, but I just gave up a rather large consulting contract with an Atlanta firm. Major personality conflicts," he said with a wave of his hand. "So, yes, absolutely yes. I'd like very much to to talk with Mr. Prickett. Ask your dad to call."

I could hardly believe it. This one could be big enough to change Dad's mind about the move. After all, he said he didn't really want to go.

"If you'll wait a few moments, I'll go down to the print room and collect some brochures and statistics on the company. It'll help in planning strategy, if we decide to do business."

He walked to the elevator, leaving the door open a few inches, while I silently thanked God for what seemed like answered prayer.

"I'm sorry if our sales representative didn't explain that to you," I heard a secretary say into the phone.

Another secretary on another phone was just ending a similar conversation. She sounded irritated at having to deal with the customer.

I knew nothing at all about insurance, but I sensed that people were not happy and not getting what they thought they had paid for. I tried to ignore the noises outside the door. I didn't want to hear more. I stood and paced the thick carpet for several minutes, trying to justify the way Mr. Brinkley was doing business.

"Okay," Junior said, pushing open the door. "Give this to your dad." He handed me a large brown envelope and offered his huge smile and another brutal handshake.

I stood in the elevator without pushing a button for a floor. I practically had the contract in my hand. Dad could sew this one up with one or two meetings. If they met in Dad's office, he'd never see the side of Brinkley Insurance that I had seen. Beads of sweat formed all along my hairline. Maybe those customers were the exception. Maybe they really should have read the fine print. I stared absent-mindedly at the fire alarm button and knew that wasn't so. No way Dad would do business with a company like this. Finally, heaving a hard sigh, I took the palm of my hand and slammed it against the first floor button.

I tossed Mr. Brinkley's large brown envelope in a trash can when I left the elevator and then hurried across the lobby. It didn't look so impressive any more. Outside the front door, two of Mr. Brinkley's employees lit up under a No Smoking sign. I brushed past them like I owned the place. I just wanted to get out of there.

"Chuck another one," I said, and climbed into the back seat of Carlos's car. "We won't be doing business with Harold Brinkley."

Scott opened his mouth to ask details, but I instantly cut him off. "I don't want to think about it anymore. Let's go to the courts."

After forty-five minutes of hard play, I was focused and breathing hard, my mind being light-years from Cleveland.

"Advantage in," I said, prepared to serve Scott the last ball of the second set. Scott waited, hunched down and moving lightly up and down on his toes, when I noticed him suddenly lower his racket and use it to gesture toward the parking lot.

"Dad?" I called, surprised.

"You about finished?"

"Uh, sure." My concentration was shot now, anyhow. "Something wrong?" I asked, my brows drawn together. Dad was seldom home at this hour, much less at the tennis courts.

He shook his head and stood waiting. I looked from Dad to Scott and back to Dad.

"Go ahead and finish," he said.

I stepped up to the service line and hit a soft shot right to Scott, and he deliberately slammed it into the net.

"Get your gear," Dad said as he turned back toward the Mustang.

I looked across at Carlos and Scott and shrugged. "See ya'."

Dad's expression was hard to read as he pulled off the side street and onto the highway leading through town.

"What?" I asked.

"Patience," he said, looking straight ahead. "I have something to show you."

I slumped down, tossed my racket to the back seat, and crossed my arms in front of me. Dad drove for fifteen minutes without saying another word. A block from his office, he turned and headed very slowly toward his building. Dad's expression was speaking volumes, but I couldn't read a word. I stared at him, almost mesmerized.

He pulled up in front of his office, parked, got out of the car, and stood leaning against the door.

I jumped out and joined him. "Dad, what's the matter? Why are we . . . ?" Then, in the dim light of early evening, I saw it. The large Prickett Small Business Consulting lettering across the front window of the office was covered with a handmade sign that read, "Prickett and Son Small Business Consulting."

I stood staring at the handmade sign with my mouth hanging partly open, unable to think of an intelligent word to say. I looked from Dad to the sign, and back to Dad again, and then broke out in a big dumb grin as I gestured toward the sign. "Does this mean that we're not? . . . I mean, what about Cleveland?"

"It means we stay in Cross Springs! The new sign goes up next week," Dad said, laying his arm across my shoulder.

"But what about the five significant contracts?"

Dad smiled. "Mike, God has been dealing with me since you started this project. You and Aunt Mof have been good examples of faith in action. I've written up thirteen small to medium contracts, made a dozen more contacts that I'll follow up on, and I've met a lot of nice people. I feel confident that God's will for us is to stay right here. I'm very proud of you, Mike."

I wanted to throw my arms around Dad in a bear hug, but in that moment, before I had time to talk myself out of it, I blurted out, "Well, Dad, you may not be so proud of me when you hear about the mess I got myself in." It was a crazy time for a confession, but I couldn't help it. I started with Scott's trip to the copy room and told Dad about the stolen exam, my efforts to return it, and then my efforts to cover up the theft. I ended with my promise to God that I'd talk to Mr. Fielder and Mrs. Valbueno and tell the truth before I took the history final.

By the time I finished the narrative, it was dark, and the cool Georgia wind had picked up. During the entire fifteen or twenty minutes that I had stood talking and staring at the sign, Dad had not moved his arm from across my shoulder.

Dad said nothing for several more minutes, and I began to relax against the door of his car, confident that I'd done the only thing I could do.

"I'm very proud of you, Mike—for telling me and for deciding to do the right thing."

Later in the evening Dad insisted that I go over the entire story again for Mom. It left her in tears, but not angry criticism.

"Mike," she said sadly, "Scott initially took the exam, but covering up a sin is not much different from the original offense."

I knew she was right.

"Well, Michael," Dad said, "we can forgive you, knowing that you've asked God for forgiveness, but as you know, all of our actions have consequences."

Here it comes, I thought, beginning to feel that cold sweaty sensation start to creep through me.

"The purpose of this punishment is only to help you take seriously the choices we all have to make. Probably the most effective way to reach you, Michael, is to restrict you from the Internet."

I held my breath, dreading his next words. This wouldn't be any one-week restriction—I could expect at least three weeks, maybe four. Four weeks without e-mail. Not to mention online conversations with Carlos and Scott.

"I'm canceling your internet provider for three months."

"But Dad . . ." I gasped. I could hardly believe what I'd heard, and immediately I wondered how I'd fill the evenings of the next three months.

As if he'd heard my thoughts, Dad said, "Maybe you'll have more time to study."

I knew better than to argue. I could only nod, as invisible tears stung my eyes. No Internet for three months. Three months. Hard to take. And the prospect of sitting in Mr. Fielder's office and admitting that I had deliberately deceived him was overwhelming.

"Would it make things easier if I set up an appointment for you boys with Mr. Fielder?" Dad asked.

Early Wednesday morning Carlos and Scott and I sat silently in Mr. Fielder's office, not moving and hardly breathing. My eyes darted around the room, remembering the family pictures on the desk and the pile of large brown envelopes and folders. Everything was exactly the same—as though he had been away for two weeks. It had been two weeks, almost to the minute, since I had slipped through the side door and out the back. I relived those moments again.

"The teacher's meeting is over. He'll be here in a minute," a helpful aide said. She closed the door.

Clenching and unclenching my fists, I worked hard to relax my upset stomach. I noticed Scott breathing hard too. Carlos seemed in a stupor, his head down, hands shoved deep in his pockets, his dark hair covering his eyes. He looked like a little kid in a great big chair.

Mr. Fielder walked briskly into his office. "Good morning boys," he said. He was followed more slowly by Mrs. Valbueno and Coach.

We responded by shifting nervously and mumbling incoherently. It was extremely humiliating to sit there, guilty, exposed to the whole school. I was glad I'd turned down Dad's offer to come along.

Mr. Fielder pulled out a chair for Mrs. Valbueno, and Coach stepped back and leaned up against the door to the copy room. He pushed his silver-rimmed glasses tightly against his nose and shifted his wad of gum.

"Mike, I talked to your dad for quite awhile yesterday, but why don't you boys start from the beginning and . . ." Mr. Fielder waved his hand in the air, inviting us to start talking.

Carlos and I looked toward Scott and gestured for him to start. He took a deep breath, lowered his head, and began what I hoped would be the last time we had to tell or hear the story. For the next fifteen minutes, the three of us talked, interrupted each other, confessed, and apologized for the stupid mess we had created. Then we sat looking at the floor, waiting.

The room was quiet for several moments. Mr. Fielder sat nodding, staring at his desk, seeming deep in thought. Mrs. Valbueno wiped tears from her eyes with a pink Kleenex. Coach studied his shoes.

"I appreciate your coming in boys, but it would have been easier if you'd come to me sooner." Mr. Fielder said slowly. "I take no pleasure in discipline, but it's necessary. Bob," he said, nodding toward Coach.

"Mike and Carlos," Coach said, "you're suspended from the team for the next quarter. Scott, two quarters—you were the one who took the exam. You'll have to compete for your places on the team after the suspension."

That's it? I thought, suspended . . . not expelled? I thanked God over and over.

But I knew there was more.

"Harriet," Mr. Fielder said, glancing at Mrs. Valbueno.

She waited until we looked up, and then went on with gathering firmness. "You boys stole a test, and then lied about it," she said, sounding indignant. "However, I do believe you regret your actions, and I believe you have repented before God."

We nodded.

"But there is a consequence for our actions."

I knew it, I knew it. *If we aren't allowed to take the history final, I'll have to repeat the course next term.*

"The exam in the morning is one hundred questions. But *you* boys will have to answer all four hundred and nine questions from your review sheet."

I tucked my head down and shoved my fists in my pockets.

"I'm sorry," Mrs. Valbueno went on, "but it's only fair."

The rest of the day my emotions bounced from the floor to the ceiling as the news of our meeting spread. I was determined to spend some time soon with Amber and tell the story one more time and explain how God had helped me to repent and confess. And as painful as the meeting in Mr. Fielder's office had been, I was relieved that we had finally told the truth. The clean, free feeling of a clear conscience was great.

After a hard match on the city courts—school courts were reserved for the team—I headed home to tell Mom and Dad about the morning meeting. (I suspected that they already knew.)

"Mikey's home," Miranda shrieked. Bikes and toys cluttered the driveway.

Suddenly, I remembered a game I used to play with my sisters. I grabbed my basketball from the garage and stood like a statue, with my arms forming a rigid circle in front of me. Then I sang out the rhyme I'd repeated for them dozens of times—but not in the last month or so. "Here's the hoop, just toss that ball. You'll make a score on every fall." For the next fifteen or twenty minutes

I pretended to be a mobile basketball hoop, making sure that every wild shot the twins threw made it through the "net." The old Mike was back. I couldn't help thinking of something Amber had said. The twins really were sort of cute.

"So, we'll leave for Cleveland on Saturday," Dad was saying as I entered my room.

"But I thought . . ." I could hardly believe what I was hearing.

"Oh, hi, Mike," Dad said. "You're home."

"We're going to Cleveland?" I asked.

"Yes, Michael . . . we're all going to Cleveland." Dad paused, then he started to smile. "For a week. We'll drive Aunt Mof home and do some sightseeing."

It took ten minutes before my breathing returned to normal. And all that time, a verse from the Youth Rally echoed through my mind: *But the salvation of the righteous is of the LORD: he is their strength in the time of trouble.*